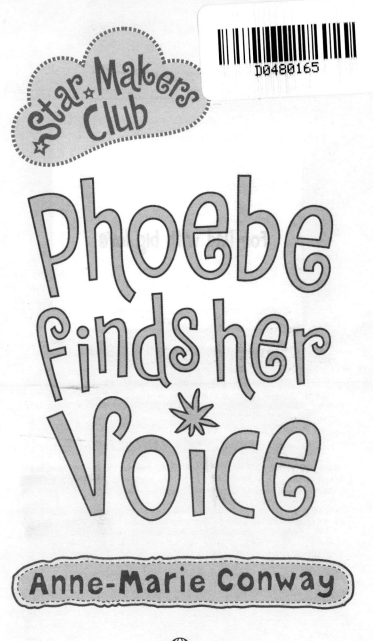

Star Makers Club

Phoebe finds her Voice

Anne-Marie Conway

USBORNE

First published in 2010 by Usborne Publishing Ltd., Usborne House,
83-85 Saffron Hill, London EC1N 8RT, England.
www.usborne.com

A CIP catalogue record for this book is available from the British Library.

JFMAMJJASO D/10   00453/2   ISBN 9781409516514
Printed in Yeovil, Somerset, UK.

The Riddle...

Everyone saw the leaflets. It was impossible not to – unless you'd been trapped in an underground cave for the past two weeks. They were everywhere: in the corridors, in the classrooms, in the dinner hall; there was even one in the girls' loo. The first one to go up was printed on bright yellow paper with a huge star in the middle. It said:

Star Makers

...is it your time to shine?

Ellie thought they'd been put up for a joke but Sam said they were from some television company looking for the next Big Thing. They were just guessing though; no one knew who'd put them up or what they were about really. And then a week later a new one appeared, stuck up in just as many places as the first. It looked exactly the same except it said:

Star Makers

...have you got what it takes?

I snagged one off the wall when no one was looking and took it home. It was like a riddle or a code or something and I was waiting for the next clue.

My name's Phoebe by the way, Phoebe Franks, and I'm nearly twelve years old. I've got flat, mousy-coloured hair – freckles, the size of saucers – and an embarrassing habit of turning beetroot every time I open my mouth. My dad's a fruitcake, my sister's a pain, and my favourite pop star of all time is Donny Dallesio. Oh yes and one more thing – I love, love, *love*, singing and dancing – but *only* when no one else is watching.

I could hear Mum clattering about in the kitchen getting breakfast ready. It was Monday morning and I had that funny feeling I always get about going back to school after the weekend, like someone's tied a knot in my tummy. It's weird because I've always loved school, and I couldn't wait to start Woodville Secondary. I was looking forward to it like mad all through Year Six – but it's been a total nightmare. It's so big, and noisy and confusing and I don't know where I am half the time – let alone where I'm supposed to be.

I pulled the duvet over my head and snuggled down for a last five minutes, thinking how brilliant it would be if I could stay under my covers for the whole day or even longer. Maybe I could teleport my bed to somewhere far away:

a different country or a different planet. Somewhere amazing where they only serve crisps for breakfast and you can eat as many packets as you like.

I closed my eyes and concentrated really hard. I tried to imagine rivers filled with salt – and smoky-bacon bushes – but it didn't work. I was still at home and I still had to go to school – and the chances of getting crisps for breakfast were about *zero*.

Downstairs Mum was sitting at the kitchen table reading something. She was hunched right over and the belt from her old, towelling dressing gown was dangling down on each side of the chair.

"The electricity bill's just arrived," she muttered as I walked in. "It's even higher than last quarter – almost double. I mean I know it's the winter, but honestly, Phoebs, how on Earth am I supposed to pay for this? We're just going to have to…"

But then she stopped, put down the electricity bill and turned into THE BREAKFAST DETECTIVE – tracking my every movement as I took a banana out of the fruit bowl.

"I'm not really hungry, Mum. It's no big deal."

"Well it is to me, Phoebe Franks," she sighed. "You're not going to school without eating a proper breakfast, and a banana is *not* a proper breakfast."

"You say that every day, but look at me, I'm fine. Do you even know how many vitamins and things there are in a banana?"

Mum gave me one of her looks and poured me a huge bowl of cornflakes.

"Oh, and I'm sorry, Phoebs, your dad phoned. He won't be able to see you on Saturday because he's got something on with his group at the centre and apparently he can't afford to miss it."

"He never can," I said, pushing my cornflakes away.

None of this surprised me, by the way. Mum always worries about the bills these days and she's always in a mood. My weirdo dad – who doesn't live at home any more – nearly always rings to say he won't be able to see me. And then there's my little sister, Sara – she just irritates the pants off of me the way that only little sisters can. I swear if you could pick and choose your family, like from one of those catalogues, she'd be going straight back.

"Something is going to happen to you today, Phoebe Franks," Sara announced suddenly, a blue and white check tea towel wrapped around her perfect blonde curls. "I've looked at your tea leaves and I'm telling you, something is going to happen – something that's going to change your life – and there's nothing you can do to stop it."

I pulled the tea towel down over her face. "I'm not drinking tea, I'm drinking orange juice, and something happens to me *every* day, raisin brain. You don't need to be a fortune-telling genius to figure that out."

"It's no use, Phoebe," Sara insisted. "You can't actually fight your own destiny, you know. Your life *is* about to change, you'll see."

"What's my destiny, then?" said Mum. "Am I going to win the lottery so I can pay some of these bills?"

"*Mum*. I can only read one fortune at a time," said Sara, dead seriously – only she didn't realize how stupid she looked sitting there with an old, stained tea towel stuck on her head.

I picked up a postcard that was lying in the middle of the table. "Hey, listen to this, Sara, it's from Gran, and she's been swimming with *real* dolphins. How cool would that be?" It was supposed to shut her up but it didn't work. Why would it? There hasn't been a thing invented yet that could shut Sara up.

"Quick, give me your hand," she squealed,

the tea towel completely covering her face. "And don't call me *Sara*, right – it's *Mystic Sara*."

She snatched the postcard away and grabbed my arm, knocking my glass over in the process. A river of sticky juice swam across the table, soaking the electricity bill, this week's shopping list and the lid of Mum's sewing box.

"For goodness' sake!" Mum snapped, whipping the tea towel off Sara's head to mop up the mess. "Don't you think I've got enough to worry about without cleaning up after you all the time? Oh it's all right for your gran, mucking about with a bunch of dolphins halfway across the world, but some of us have to work for a living!"

And while they argued about spilled juice and dolphins and telling fortunes, I sneaked a packet of crisps out of the cupboard and escaped back upstairs to my bedroom.

We always walk to school whatever the

weather; it's only three roads away. Our road is very long and full of squashed-together houses that all look exactly the same, so if all the numbers disappeared or blew away or something, you could easily end up going into the wrong house.

We have to shoot past Number Four as fast as we can; Valerie – *beaky-nose* – Burton lives there, with her frizzy bird's-nest hair and lips as thin as string. She's got this creepy way of appearing out of nowhere, like in a **HORROR MOVIE**, and once she's got a hold of you it's impossible to get away.

She goes on and on about the **state of the country** and the **state of the education system** and she especially likes to go on about **broken homes** where the *poor* children never get to see their dads – meaning me and Sara, of course.

It's the children I feel sorry for, she always says, looking at us and nodding like crazy – until I think her head might actually drop off.

I hope it does one day. I hope it drops off and rolls away!

When we get to Sara's school, Mum goes in with Sara and I carry on by myself down one more very long road and then round the corner to Woodville Secondary. I don't know why it's called *Wood*ville; it's surrounded by these tall, grey railings – like a prison – and there isn't a tree in sight.

It was one of those freezing cold mornings, the kind when you can see the breath coming out of your mouth. Outside the school gates, Polly Carter was standing with one of her pathetic little sidekicks, holding a pencil and pretending to smoke. I tried to stay out of her way, but just before we went in she pushed past me and hissed, "Watch where you're going, *Phoebe*, can't you!" as if it was all my fault in the first place.

She's such a witch, Polly Carter. She's been on my case ever since I joined Woodville in

September but I've got no idea why. Hate at first sight or something. I was just about to ask her where she'd left her broomstick – but the bell rang and everyone trooped inside.

I noticed the third leaflet straight away. It was stuck up right next to our lockers and I nearly dropped my bag when I saw what it said.

Star Makers
...is your life about to change?

Seriously, I'm not kidding. It totally spooked me out – like Sara really could see into the future. I spent the whole day waiting for something to happen, *anything*, but it was pretty much business as usual. In maths we learned some complicated new way of doing long division, but since I can't do the old way there wasn't really much hope I was going to get the new one. Then in English, as part of our poetry topic, we had to write a humorous limerick.

I love writing – especially poems – but when Mr. Davis asked if anyone wanted to read theirs out to the class I looked down at my desk and pretended to be busy sharpening one of my pencils.

"Put your hand up, Phoebs," hissed Ellie, leaning over and reading mine. "It's wicked!" But I couldn't, not in a million years, and by the end of the lesson my pencil was so sharp I could've used it to pierce Polly Carter's ears.

The trouble with me is that I'm shy – and I'm not talking about the way some children are shy, like when they walk into a room full of total strangers, or have to speak out loud in assembly. I'm talking about being so shy that sometimes I can't speak at all. The words are there, squashed inside my head, but it's like I don't know how to get them out any more.

I didn't used to be shy – just the opposite – but ever since Dad left *and* since I started at Woodville, it's like I've had a personality transplant or something. Sometimes I wonder if maybe I left my *old* personality at Merryhill Primary. That if I popped in there one day – after dropping Sara off in the morning – I'd find it hidden behind a radiator, or stuffed down one of the loos.

Anyway, by the end of the day, after double science and the most boring French lesson ever, I'd more or less forgotten about Sara's prediction at breakfast. Then just as we were getting ready to go home, our form teacher, Miss Howell, said she had something important to tell us. I stopped sorting through my stack of homework and looked up.

She was standing at the front of the classroom with some bright yellow leaflets in her hand – *the* bright yellow leaflets – and she looked excited, like it was her birthday, or she'd won the lottery or something. It's not like I even believe in fortune-telling, I'm not that stupid, but there was something about the way she was standing there, with that look on her face, holding those mysterious leaflets, that made me wonder, just for a second, if The Great *Mystic* Sara might have been right after all.

2
How Tiny Little Things Can End Up Really BIG!

"Just stop what you're doing and listen up for a minute, guys," said Miss Howell, waving the leaflets about. "I've got some really exciting news." She ran her hand through her hair. It was short and black with a bright pink streak down the middle.

"Are you getting married then, Miss?" Patrick Thornton shouted out. "Are those the invitations?"

She grinned. "No, I'm not getting married, Patrick, but don't worry, if I was, you'd be right up there at the top of my guest list."

I stared at the leaflets. I didn't know what Miss Howell was going to say or what they were about but I just knew it was going to be something exciting. I held my breath and waited.

"It's a drama club," announced Miss Howell. "I've decided to start an out-of-school drama club called Star Makers on Saturday mornings. We'll be doing heaps of drama games, lots of singing and dancing, and then in February we're going to put on a big musical production that I've written myself, called *The Dream Factory*."

My heart started to race. I'd always wanted to join a drama club – and if Miss Howell was in charge I knew it would be good. She's our drama teacher as well as our form teacher and she's brilliant. She's really young and trendy and her drama lessons are the best. I look forward to them all week even though I usually end up hiding at the back, terrified she might choose me to do something in front of the class.

Of course at Merryhill I would've been the first one up there, showing off in front of everyone. I even had a solo in our end-of-year production. I remember Mum and Dad came to watch – *together* – and when I ran on for my bow I could hear them cheering and whistling louder than anyone.

"But why did you stick all those leaflets up?" Tara – *brains of the class* – Perkins called out suddenly, her hand shooting up in the air. "I've spent the past two weeks trying to guess what they were about; it's been driving me nuts. Why didn't you just hand the leaflets out?"

"For exactly that reason, Tara," said Miss Howell, laughing. "I wanted to get your attention. I wanted to get everyone talking and it worked! But I am going to hand the leaflets out today. The first session is next Saturday, so if any of you think you might like to join – and it *is* going to be very special – take a leaflet and show it to Mum or Dad as soon as you get home."

I held on to mine tight, reading it over and

over; wanting to join more than anything but knowing I'd never be brave enough. When the bell rang I trailed outside and gave the leaflet to Mum. It was all crumpled up and my hand felt horribly hot and sweaty.

"Hey, this sounds great, Phoebe, and you know, it would probably do you the world of good. You've been so quiet since...since..." Mum trailed off, fussing with the buttons on Sara's coat. She was going to say, *since Dad left*, that I've been so quiet since my dad left home – but she likes to pretend that nothing's changed, that Dad still lives at home and everything's the same as it used to be.

"It sounds all right," I said slowly, "but, look, it's way too expensive, Mum. You said we couldn't even afford the electricity bill this morning. And anyway, I see Dad on Saturdays, don't I."

Mum glanced back down at the leaflet. "Don't worry about that, Phoebs; it's not very expensive at all compared to some of those other drama clubs you hear about. Anyway, I'm sure Gran will pay if it's something you really want to do and it's only for a few hours in the morning, so you'd still be able to see your dad in the afternoons."

And then Sara started. Bleating away like some sort of whiny goat. "Oh, but I want to go too, Mum. And you know how brilliant I am at singing, *pleeeease*."

"You can't go," I said. "You're too young, you have to be ten and you're only eight, and anyway I don't want to go either, so let's just go home."

"Come on, Phoebs, what's the matter?" Mum put her arm round me and gave me one of her looks. "You've always loved singing and dancing. You and Ellie used to spend every spare minute in your room making up plays together. This would be such a great opportunity for you."

I knew she was right but that just made me feel worse. I shook off her arm and walked away. I wanted to join, of course I did, but there was no way I'd be able to act or sing or anything like that, not in front of Miss Howell and the others.

Back at home, Sara plonked herself down on the sofa to watch TV and Mum got busy sewing. During the week she does shifts at the Co-op on the High Road, but in the evenings and on Saturdays she makes dresses for people, like bridesmaids' dresses and christening dresses. She's brilliant at sewing but she's always totally stressed about getting stuff finished on time, so I knew there was no point trying to talk to her.

I did some homework, and ate my tea, and tried my best not to think about Star Makers. I wasn't going to join so there was no use tormenting myself. It would probably be stuffed full of loud-mouth show-offs anyway, all tripping over themselves to get the best parts and Miss Howell would have to get an extra wide door fitted for all their big heads to squeeze through. Anyone a little bit quiet or shy like me would end up getting trampled on or squashed and Miss Howell wouldn't even notice because all the others would drown out my cries for help – showing off about how amazing and super-talented they were.

Who'd want to go to something like that anyway? I'd had a lucky escape. I could join a karate club instead – that would be far more useful. I'd be able to sort Polly Carter out for a start. I wouldn't even have to say anything; I'd just finish her off with a knee strike and a deadly upper-hold or whatever the moves are called.

I practised a few kicks in the middle of my room and had Polly lying on the floor begging for mercy when Ellie rang.

"Hi, Phoebs."

"Oh, hi, Ellie. Have you done your Literacy yet?"

"Erm...no, I lost the sheet on the way home. I dropped it as I was leaving school and it blew away. It's probably halfway to France by now," she giggled.

"Not again, Ellie. Mr. Davis will go spare."

"I know, I know, but it was really windy and I was carrying way too many things. Anyway, listen, Phoebs, Sam just texted me, and we're both going to join Miss Howell's drama club. So are you going to come?"

Sam Lester – biggest show-off of all time – and Ellie's new *best friend*. Ellie and I have been best friends ever since nursery, but I swear the minute we got to Woodville, she had a good look around and managed to find the loudest person in the whole, entire year group to hang out with.

"Phoebe, are you listening? I said are you going to come?"

"No, I mean yes, I mean *yes* I am listening but *no*, I can't come. My mum says it's way too expensive. She won't even get me a phone until Christmas so she's not about to pay for a drama club."

"It's not *that* expensive, is it? Look, why don't I get my mum to ring your mum and see if she can talk her round?"

"No, it's fine, Ellie, honest. I don't even want to join. I'm going to start karate lessons on Saturdays so I won't have time anyway."

"*Karate lessons?* Since when have you been interested in karate, Phoebs? This could be our chance to put on a *real* show!"

"Yeah I know, but listen Ellie, Mum's calling me. Better go. Speak later."

I'm always doing that – making things up quickly to get out of a tricky situation, and then getting found out and feeling stupid. I don't think of it as lying exactly, just a way of covering up how shy I am and how a little thing like going to a drama club can end up *really* BIG in my head.

I lay down on my bed and stared up at my favourite poster of Donny Dallesio. He's wearing this white suit and doing a double thumbs up with the biggest grin on his face. I stared into his deep, brown eyes wondering how everything got to be such a mess. I bet if he was here, right this second, he'd say, "Stop being such a wimp, Phoebe Franks and tell your mum you want to join." But he wasn't here and anyway, even if the words were there inside my head, there's no way I'd ever be able to get them out.

I lay there for ages thinking about singing and dancing and Ellie and Sam, and Star Makers – about how I *did* want to join, more than anything, if only I wasn't so scared. Then, just when I thought I couldn't stand thinking about it any more, something totally weird happened. Donny stretched his arm right out of the poster – *yes, right out of it* – and gave *me* a 'thumbs up'.

I blinked really hard and then blinked again and the poster was back to normal. My heart started to race. I sat up straight. I was obviously losing it – big time – unless it was a sign! I thought about what Sara had said at breakfast – about how my life was about to change – and before I could bottle out or do anything stupid, I tore downstairs and told Mum that I did want to join Star Makers Drama Club after all.

Thumbs Up For Phoebe!

Okay, fine. So I said I'd *join* Star Makers, but I didn't say I'd actually *go*. I tried ringing Ellie early on Saturday morning to see if she could pick me up – the last thing I wanted to do was walk in by myself – but she'd already arranged to go with Sam. So then I tried to come up with some really good reasons not to go at all. Like maybe I should spend my Saturdays doing extra maths so that I didn't fall behind, or maybe Saturday would be the perfect day for me to spend more time with Sara. We could bake biscuits and dress up her Barbie dolls.

"*Play Barbies with Sara?*" Mum snorted, when I told her. "Listen to me, Phoebe, you really need to get out and make some new friends. Come on, get your coat. Your dad will be here in a sec and I want you ready to go."

So I didn't end up walking in by myself after all. I got to walk in with my saddo dad, who went on and on all the way there about how happy he was that I was *coming out of my shell* and *joining in with other children* – like I was two or something. And then who was the first person I saw standing in the middle of the hall staring at me with her witch-green eyes and scrunched-up face? My favourite person in the Whole Entire Universe – Polly Carter.

I grabbed Dad's hand and tried to turn back towards the door, but unfortunately Miss Howell came straight over to us before I could make a run for it. She looked amazing. She dyes her hair a different colour practically every week and it was jet black with bright yellow tips, sticking up like the spikes on a hedgehog.

"Phoebe, hi, it's *so* great to see you. Come

and stand over here with me in the circle, we're just about to start some warm-up games. Oh, and Mr. Franks, if you could fill out a form – they're in a pile over there on the piano – that would be great."

I had a quick look round. There were loads of children, all talking and messing about – some from Woodville and some from other schools. The hall itself was pretty ordinary. I'd half expected it to look like a proper theatre with special lights and fancy seats and stuff but it wasn't like that at all. At one end there was a huge, wooden stage with heavy-looking, blue velvet curtains. Then just in front of the stage there was an ancient piano that looked as if it was about to collapse at any moment, but apart from that and a stack of chairs it was empty.

I stood next to Miss Howell in the circle but kept my eyes fixed firmly on Dad filling out the form. I was trapped in a room with Polly Carter and I didn't know what to do. I stared at Dad's back, trying desperately to communicate telepathically that I wanted him to take me home. But it didn't work. Of course it didn't. I mean we don't even communicate *non*-telepathically these days.

He finished the form in double quick time, mouthed *'see you later'* and disappeared through the double doors. I stood totally still to stop myself from running straight after him. Tara Perkins from my class was standing next to me in the circle.

"I didn't know you were coming, Phoebe," she said, peering at me through her little round glasses.

"Nor did I actually, Tara," I felt like saying. "Not until Donny Dallesio more or less tricked me into joining." But of course I didn't say that at all, I just gave her one of my best twisted-up smiles and mumbled, "Hi."

Ellie waved at me from the other side of the circle. She was wearing a new top and her thick, glossy hair was dead straight like she'd used straighteners on it. Sam was next to her and she was wearing exactly the same top. In fact, even though Sam's hair is blonde and curly and Ellie's is dark brown, they looked like clones or something – standing there like that in their matching tops.

Next to Ellie on her other side was a boy with sticking-up red hair – not ginger, but bright red like a postbox. My heart started to thud. I looked away and then looked back. It couldn't be. *It couldn't.* But even with his hair dyed that ridiculous colour, I knew it was: Montgomery Brown, also known as Monty B, my ex-next-door-neighbour and Most Irritating Person Ever.

Monty B lived next door to us for years; I think I was only four when he moved in. He used to call me Frankie and he was over at ours all the time like he thought we were best friends.

He grinned at me across the circle but I looked away, my face burning up. He moved out of our road about two years ago, and I don't even know why but seeing him here after so long was more embarrassing than anything.

"Before we get started," Miss Howell was saying, "I want to have a little chat with you about Star Makers, and about what I'm hoping we can achieve here." She looked at each one of us around the circle.

"Star Makers is *not* about being the best or getting the biggest parts," she said, serious for a moment. "Star Makers is all about being part of a group; a special group, where everyone is important and everyone has their moment to shine."

"But some people will get big parts won't they?" Sam called out.

"Of course some people will have bigger parts than others, Sam, but as each of you grows in confidence, over time, your turn to have the biggest part will come."

Sam looked a bit disappointed. She probably thought she was going to get the biggest part every time.

"Now let's start with some name games," said Miss Howell. "Oh, and talking of names, I'd really like the children who go to Woodville to call me Mandy while we're at drama."

"That will be so weird, won't it?" whispered Tara. "Calling Miss Howell, Mandy."

But I couldn't answer. I was too busy working out how I was going to escape – from Polly Carter *and* Monty B.

"We're going to go round the circle and when it gets to your turn I want you to say your name and do an action at the same time," said Miss Howell. "It can be any sort of action you feel like: a clap, a stamp, a kick, anything at all – and then everyone else will repeat that person's name and copy the action."

Say my name? Do an action? *In front of*

strange people?! I really had to get out of there and fast.

"Oh, can I start, Mandy?" Sam called out, but before Miss Howell could even answer she kicked one of her legs high up into the air and shouted, "I'm Sam, yes I am!" like she was a Dr. Seuss character or something. Ellie was next. She said her name and then burst into giggles, so everyone said her name and giggled back. Then it was Monty B's turn. He yelled "Monty B!" did a flying cartwheel right across the circle and landed in a heap at my feet.

I couldn't tell you what anyone else did after that. I desperately wanted to make a run for it, but I knew that if I moved or spoke or even breathed something horrible would happen.

As Tara Perkins finished her go twenty pairs of eyes turned towards me like deadly lasers and I wished more than anything that I *could* drop dead – or magic myself back home with Mum. I didn't think I was going to say or do anything at all. I was pretty sure that even if I tried to speak no sound would come out of my mouth.

But then something clicked in my head like an invisible switch turning on and this picture of Donny appeared, as clear as if he was standing right in front of me. He was grinning wildly and doing a double thumbs up just like in my poster – and before I could even think about what I was going to do next, I said "Phoebe Franks" in the tiniest whisper – I doubt anyone even heard it – and *I* did a double thumbs up.

For a minute I couldn't believe I'd spoken out loud. Maybe I'd imagined the whole thing, like in my bedroom. But then everyone else shouted out "*Phoebe Franks!*" and did a double thumbs up, and the game carried on around the circle. I wiped my sweaty palms on the back of my jeans, said a silent *thank you* to Donny and breathed again.

When the circle games were finished, Miss Howell asked us to walk around the hall using all the available space. I tried to stay as near to Ellie as I could without making it obvious. But she kept changing direction and she was walking so fast she was almost running, so it was more or less impossible for me to keep up with her.

In the end I gave up and walked around by myself. I was just thinking about how much I wanted to go home and about how amazing it was that one measly morning could somehow seem like a whole entire week, when Polly Carter walked past me with two of her mates from school.

"All right, Phoebe Franks," she said, sarcastically, giving me a thumbs up. She looked back at her friends sniggering, but before I could answer – or stick my thumb in her eye – Miss Howell shouted "Freeze!"

"Right, guys, get into groups of four with

whoever you're standing closest to," she called out from the front. "And I don't want to see anyone running across the hall to be with their friends!"

Of course Ellie was nowhere in sight, and I wasn't about to go with Polly, so I shuffled over to Tara from my class – at least she was someone I knew. Then this really funny girl called Neesha who lives in Ellie's road came over – and so did Monty B.

"Hey, Frankie," he said, lifting his hand up for a high five.

I looked at him, horrified. "Don't call me Frankie here," I hissed. "And why on earth is your hair bright red?"

His face lit up as if I'd paid him a massive compliment or something. "Oh, it was kind of like a dare that went wrong," he said. "I thought it would wash out but I bought the wrong stuff and it turns out it was permanent. My dad hit the roof big time – but Mum said it was an expression of my individuality – you know what she's like."

"*An expression of your individuality?*" snorted Neesha, rolling her eyes and grinning at me. "What are you – a traffic light?"

"Very funny, Neesha. But did you know that, statistically speaking, people with red hair are more likely to succeed than people with brown hair like yours?"

"So you'll be a really successful traffic light!" said Neesha. "Congratulations."

I sneaked a look at Monty B while they were talking, but he caught me peeking and winked at me. I couldn't believe he was the same annoying little boy I used to ride my bike with, and roll down the hill in the park with, and do other horribly embarrassing things that I didn't even want to think about.

We did loads more games in our groups, had a quick break, and then Miss Howell called us over to the piano to teach us a song.

"The auditions for *The Dream Factory* will actually be next Saturday," she said, handing round some sheets with the words on. "I know it doesn't give you much time to prepare but we're going to be performing the show in February, so I'd really like to get going. This is the song I want you to learn for the singing audition. It's..."

"Oh, I just *love* auditions," cried Sam. "I did this audition once and I was nearly chosen to be on telly. It was *so* amazing."

Personally I couldn't see what was so great about *nearly* being chosen to be on telly, but then Sam has this way of making everything she does sound like it's *so* amazing.

"It's sung by Sabine right at the beginning of the show," Miss Howell went on, giving Sam a look. "Sabine is one of the main characters. She lives in the factory with the Sweet-Dreamers, who make all our *sweet* dreams, and the Jelly-Skulls, who make all our nightmares. Her parents, Baron-Von-Bolt and Ice Bomb, run the factory and they're really cruel to her. They treat her like a servant – kind of like Cinderella – so this song is all about how wretched her life is."

Name games and thumbs up and audition songs – I didn't know what I was doing there, or why I ever thought I was the sort of person who could join a drama club, let alone audition for a part in a show. Talk about nightmares and wretched lives. There was no way I was going to come back – not in a million years.

But then Miss Howell started to play Sabine's song on the piano and, by the time she'd played it through twice, all that other stuff had flown straight out of my head. I don't even know why, or how, or what happened, but it was as if Sabine's song had cast a spell over me.

So what if I was Phoebe Franks, *World's Shyest Person*? So what if Sabine was one of the biggest parts in the show? So what if I could barely say my name in front of the others, let alone sing a solo? I knew in that instant – as the music filled my head – that I *had* to be Sabine, no matter what.

The Extra Place...

As soon as we got home, I left Mum and Dad arguing on the doorstep and raced up to my room to start practising. Whenever Dad drops us back on a Saturday they end up shouting at each other. Well, Mum shouts and Dad just stands there, which totally winds Mum up and makes her shout even more. They argue about me and Sara and arrangements and money and a whole load of other boring stuff.

I usually hide under my covers with my earphones in until Dad leaves, but today I sat on my bed and sang Sabine's song to drown them out. Miss Howell had given us the *Dream Factory* script and I could still hear the tune playing in my head. I sang it through three or four times, getting louder and louder, as Mum started screaming at Dad and Sara started to wail. Then I grabbed a hairbrush to be my microphone and stood in front of my full-length mirror to sing it again – even louder.

I felt so different up in my room where no one could see me, it was like magic, and for a few minutes I was right there, in that wretched factory, singing about how tragic my life was. I didn't only sound like Sabine, I *was* Sabine. I couldn't even hear Mum and Dad arguing any more – it was as if they didn't exist – but then suddenly there was an almighty bang from downstairs – and the spell was broken.

I looked at myself in the mirror and saw my reflection. I mean *really* saw it. I saw how flat my hair was, stuck to my ears like overcooked spaghetti, and how completely stupid I looked standing there pretending to be a singer. *And* how stupid I must have looked standing in the circle at drama doing that pathetic thumbs-up sign. I flopped down on my bed in despair. If I was ever going to convince Miss Howell in a million years that I was the right person to be Sabine, I needed to make some changes – and fast.

Suddenly my door flew open and Sara burst in, sobbing.

"Quick, Phoebe! *Quick*! Mum shut the door in Dad's face and I think it hit his nose. It might be broken or squashed or bleeding and Mrs. Burton was standing outside listening to everything they said and—"

"Wait a sec, how do you know that – about Mrs. Burton?"

"Because she came over to tell Mum to keep the noise down and that's when Mum slammed the door."

"Well Mum was probably trying to squash Mrs. Burton's nose, and Dad's nose just got in the way."

Sara always works herself up into such a state when Mum and Dad argue – like she still expects them to be best friends or something.

"Anyway, noses are harder than you think," I added to calm her down a bit. "Especially grown-ups' noses."

She wiped her snotty face on her sleeve. "Are you sure?" she said, and sat down on the end of my bed as if she was planning to stay for a while.

"Yes, I'm sure, Sara, *really*. But can you get out now?" I shoved her with my foot. "I was right in the middle of something vitally important and you didn't knock."

"*Of course I didn't knock!*" she cried dramatically. "It was an actual emergency in case you didn't notice." And she slammed out of the room leaving me to get on with my plan.

So somehow by next Saturday I had to transform myself into a tragic heroine with the confidence to sing in front of the entire drama group – but how? I mean let's face it; it's not as if a fairy godmother was going to appear in my room waving a magic wand about any time soon. And then it came to me. It was so obvious. What I needed was a makeover.

I suddenly got this picture in my head, as clear as anything, of Monty B and his traffic-light hair. I wasn't going to dye my hair bright red, I wasn't *that* stupid, but I had to do *something* to change my image. Something to make Miss Howell think *I* was the Sabine she was looking for!

I leaned over and dragged a pile of magazines out from underneath my bed. They were stuffed full of articles about Donny Dallesio – and I remembered in one of them there was a brilliant interview he gave ages ago about how he'd transformed himself from a shy, geeky-looking teenager, into a world-famous superstar. I started leafing through as fast as I could; there was literally no time to lose.

I found articles about his childhood and his favourite foods and his star sign. There was even one about his **BIG TOE** – which was apparently misshapen at birth and had to be operated on when he was ten. But I couldn't see anything about this Great Transformation. And then just as I was about to give up, in the very last magazine, I found it:

"My Rise to Fame" – by Donny Dallesio

It was a really long article and most of it was no use at all, but there was one section about his hair – called Gel Spell – that looked quite interesting, and one about his special "stage smile" – called the Razzle Dazzle. I read that section first. I mean anyone could learn how to smile, couldn't they?

"The **Razzle Dazzle Smile** is a smile that shows **ALL** your teeth," it said. "Think Hollywood! Think Toothpaste Ad! Think

Crocodile! A smile is the singer's disguise. A smile will hide the fact that you might be tired or sad or downright terrified. Smile, my friends, and the whole world will smile with you.

"Perfecting the Razzle Dazzle Smile took many months of practice but once I'd mastered the technique I knew I was on my way. Future stars of the stage and screen – never forget the Razzle Dazzle Smile. It worked for me and it could work for you."

Months to perfect??? I didn't have months to practise a stupid smile. Surely it couldn't be that difficult – except I've always been rubbish at smiling even when I'm happy. My smiles come out all weird and twisted and sometimes they don't come out at all.

I tried to smile in the mirror but it looked awful; like I had some manky disease that affected the muscles around my mouth. I tried again but it looked even worse. I was just about to try singing *and* smiling at the same time when the phone rang.

"Come and talk to your gran, Phoebe," Mum shouted up the stairs, "and then it's time to eat."

I trailed downstairs thinking about the Razzle Dazzle Smile, and about how I had less than seven days to get it right. Mum was in the kitchen. She handed me the phone and carried on making tea.

"Hello, Gran."

"Hello, Phoebe, sweetheart. Did you survive the dreaded drama club?"

"Just about, Gran. It was good. A bit scary – well very – but good."

"Did you know many people?"

"Erm, Polly Carter was there, worst luck, and Ellie and Sam. Oh, and you won't believe it but Monty B was there. You know; our old next-door neighbour."

"Oh, I remember Monty B. He was a lovely little boy. Was it nice to see him?"

"Not really. He's not little any more and he's definitely not lovely. His hair is bright red like a traffic light and he kept following me around. Anyway, we're putting on this show, called *The Dream Factory*. And we learned this song that Sabine sings, she's the main character, and it's so cool. I've been practising ever since I got home. But then...but then..."

"But then *what*, love?"

I could imagine Gran's creased-up, worried face at the other end of the phone.

"Oh, nothing. Then the phone rang, that's all."

"Well, you just wait until that Miss Howell of yours hears what a fantastic voice you've got. She won't believe her ears. I've got to go now but you've no idea how much I miss you. I'll come down and see you as soon as I can. Oh and Phoebe, love, how's Mum today?"

I glanced at Mum. She looked awful.

"She's fine," I lied. "Take care, Gran. Bye."

"Can you give me a hand with these drinks?" Mum said, when I'd put the phone down. "It's teatime. And when you've done that, go and get Sara, would you? She's upstairs having a strop about Dad's nose or something."

I carried the cups over to the table. There were four.

"Who's coming to tea?" I asked, a funny feeling growing in my stomach. "Why have you laid the table for four? Who's coming?"

Mum whipped round as if I'd slapped her and snatched the extra cup out of my hand.

"Just go and get Sara," she said. Her voice was rock hard.

"You forgot, didn't you?" I said. "You forgot *again*."

"For goodness' sake, Phoebe! I don't want to talk about it. Now go and get Sara."

"I'm already here!" cried Sara suddenly, standing at the door clutching her favourite teddy, Barney. "And stop shouting, can't you?"

she said, clamping her hands over Barney's ears. "You know Barney doesn't like it."

Mum turned back to the sink, but not before I saw her eyes fill with tears. She did it every few weeks, laid the table for four instead of three. It was for Dad. She laid it for my dad. And every time she did, I felt as if someone had punched me really hard.

The extra place wasn't mentioned again, but Mum barely looked at me all through tea and I couldn't wait to get back upstairs. I wasn't sure about the Razzle Dazzle Smile – I didn't really feel like smiling – but there was nothing to stop me practising Sabine's song. I knew I couldn't get Mum to be happy, or get my dad to be normal again, or get Polly Carter to leave me alone. But that didn't mean I couldn't get the part of Sabine.

5

Popcorn Round at Dad's

I practised Sabine's song every spare minute. I practised it in my room and in the bath and on the way to school in my head. I practised it so much I began to think I *was* Sabine, living in that dreary Dream Factory with her cruel parents. Ellie and Sam had practised loads as well and they both sounded brilliant, especially Sam.

"I just really hope I'm brave enough to audition," said Ellie at school on Wednesday. We were in the playground at lunchtime talking about Star Makers and the auditions and about how much all three of us were dying to be Sabine.

"I don't know what you're so scared about,

Ellie," said Sam. "I can't wait until Saturday. I could give you some tips if you like." She jumped up in front of us. "First of all you have to stand with your legs apart and your shoulders back like this, and it's really important that you don't fidget."

"But you know what I'm like," moaned Ellie. "I can't keep still for more than two seconds."

"Well, you'll have to practise," said Sam. "The other thing to remember is to make eye contact with Miss Howell and to show her that you really understand the meaning of the song. Like, it's no use looking happy if the song is sad like Sabine's song is."

I thought about Donny and his Razzle Dazzle Smile but I didn't say anything.

"Oh yeah, and you have to open your mouth properly. That's mega. If you don't open your mouth really wide you won't make a loud enough sound even if you've got a good voice."

Sam *always* had her mouth wide open, so I

was sure that wouldn't be too much of a problem for her.

"But listen, Ellie, if you're too scared to try out for a main part," she went on, "why don't you audition to be one of the Sweet-Dreamers? You always have the weirdest dreams anyway, so that part would be perfect for you."

"I actually had the weirdest dream ever last night," said Ellie. "I was standing on the stage about to audition for the show when this dinosaur burst in to the room and gobbled everyone up except for me and Miss Howell. It was a T. Rex, I think. The funny thing was, Miss Howell didn't seem to be upset or shocked or anything. She just said, "Oh, well done, Ellie. I guess that means *you're* going to be Sabine.""

Sam snorted. "I'd carry on practising if I were you," she said. "I don't think there's much chance of a dinosaur turning up on Saturday. How about you, Phoebe? Are you ready to audition?"

"Phoebe's got a brilliant voice," said Ellie. "You should hear her, Sam."

But just then Sam went charging off across the playground after some Year Nine boy she fancies and I was left wondering if she ever *would* hear me sing – or if I'd be too scared when it got to Saturday.

The next day, Dad and Sara came to pick me up from school. Mum had some bridesmaids' dresses to finish, so we were going over to Dad's for tea. They were waiting for me outside the gates, their heads close together chatting. Dad was wearing his scruffy PEACE NOW T-shirt, some awful brown sandals and his fake smile.

He's been smiling like that ever since he moved out; like he thinks if he sticks a smile on his face we won't realize what a mess everything is. Sometimes I think I could reach up and peel that smile right off like a plaster, and underneath his real mouth would be all turned down and sad.

"We're going to make popcorn, Phoebs!" cried Sara, when she saw me. She started to hop about like a demented rabbit. "Dad said we could make popcorn and watch a DVD like we're in a real cinema. Barney absolutely loves popcorn," she gabbled on, pulling Barney out of her book bag and whispering something in his ear. I grabbed hold of her and pushed her down the road. The last thing I wanted was Polly Carter to show up and see my loopy sister talking to her teddy – *or* my dad in his manky sandals.

Back at the flat, Dad and Sara got busy in the kitchen. There wasn't really room for all three of us so I went to sit in the lounge. It was practically empty except for a tatty, old couch and a few boxes Dad hadn't got round to unpacking yet.

Mum and Dad split up ninety-two days ago – not that I'm counting or anything. Mum said that Dad had gone strange in the head and she couldn't live with his crazy ideas any more. Well, okay, she didn't use those words exactly, but she's right, he has gone strange in the head, especially since he lost his job and joined the $\mathcal{L}$ife centre. He used to work at this amazing nursery where they grew all sorts of rare, tropical plants. He'd worked there for years and years, ever since he left school – but then out of the blue they said they were cutting back the staff or something and that he'd have to leave.

At first he didn't do much at all, just moped about the house watching rubbish TV all day. But then after about six months he went and joined this weird New Age group called $\mathcal{L}$ife. He goes to the $\mathcal{L}$ife centre all the time now, especially on Saturdays when he's supposed to be with me and Sara. I don't even know what they do there – but it's obviously more exciting than being with us.

The popcorn was taking ages so I decided to try out Sam's great audition tips while I was waiting. I stood in the middle of the living room with my legs apart and my shoulders back and pretended Miss Howell was sitting in front of me on the couch. I reached my arm out towards her, took a deep breath, opened my mouth as wide as I could and was just about to start singing when Sara burst in.

"*What's the matter?*" she squealed, staring at where my hand was pointing. "*Did you see a spider or something?*"

I dropped my arm, and spun round. "For goodness' sake, Sara! Don't creep up on me like that! What do you want anyway?"

"I was just gonna tell you about the popcorn." She grinned. "We've made so much it's flying around all over the place. It's brilliant. We're going to put butter and salt on it, but you can have yours plain if you want. Come on!"

In the kitchen the popcorn was banging about inside the pan and Dad was standing next to the stove grinning and looking very pleased with himself.

"Bet you didn't know I could make popcorn, eh, Phoebe?" he said, as if it was some amazingly rare talent that only two or three people in the whole world could do.

"Isn't this *brilliant*, Phoebe!" said Sara again, hopping around the kitchen. And just for that second, looking at Sara's happy, shining face, it was brilliant.

I trailed back into the living room, still thinking about the audition. Dad came in a couple of minutes later carrying two big bowls of buttery popcorn.

"How was drama on Saturday, Phoebe? I never got the chance to ask you."

"Of course you didn't get the chance to ask me," I felt like saying, "you were too busy rowing with Mum." But I didn't say anything.

I just sat down cross-legged on the worn-out carpet and shrugged.

"It wasn't that great," I said in the end. "I might start karate instead."

"*Karate?* But Phoebe, you've got such a lovely singing voice. Remember what I used to say to you when you were little? That you were *born* to be on the stage."

I hugged my bowl of popcorn. Of course I remembered and maybe I *was* born to be on the stage – but that was before everything went wrong. Before Dad left, and before I started at Woodville Secondary, and before Polly Carter decided to ruin my life.

"Anyway, I *can't* go back!" I blurted out suddenly. "We've got to do this stupid audition and I'll never be able to do it, not in a million years!" The words tumbled out of my mouth. I wanted him to know that nothing was the same any more: that I wasn't the same little girl who used to sing and dance around the living room.

"Sam says I have to stand in a certain way and Donny Dallesio says in this magazine that you have to smile showing all your teeth, and I don't even know if I can sing in front of Miss Howell and all the others in the first place, so there's no way I'm going to be able to sing and smile *and* stand properly all at the same time. It's totally hopeless and I'm quitting, *okay?*"

Dad looked a bit shocked. It was easily the most I'd said to him for about a year.

"Well, *we* could tell you if you're any good, Phoebs," said Sara, coming in. She was carrying a huge bowl of popcorn for her and a tiny little one for Barney. "Just pretend it's *X Factor* or something and we're the judges. Dad can be—"

"I'm not singing in front of you," I said, horrified.

"Come on, Phoebe," said Dad. "Sara's right. If you have a go here you'll feel more confident on Saturday. Forget about what Sam said and about what you read in that magazine. Just sit there on the carpet and sing the song."

"There's no way! I can't! You'll just laugh, I know you will."

"We won't!" cried Sara. "We won't even look, promise." She plonked herself down next to Dad and put her hands over Barney's eyes.

"Come on, Phoebe," said Dad, smiling. "I'd really love to hear you sing."

I looked at the three of them, Dad, Sara and Barney, the bear, lined up on the couch with their eyes closed tight, clutching their bowls of buttery popcorn – and I knew Dad was right. If I couldn't sing here, in front of my own family, there was no way I'd ever be able to audition in front of everyone at drama.

"Do you swear on your life you won't laugh?"

"Cross my heart and hope to die," said Dad.

"Cross my heart and hope *you* die!" said Sara.

"Well...okay... I'll sing a bit," I said, ignoring Sara. "But the second you open your eyes or laugh or even smile I'm going to stop."

They sat completely still right through the song. After a bit I forgot they were even there and I sang the way I always sing when I'm by myself in my bedroom. They didn't even move after I'd finished. They just sat there staring at me. But then suddenly Dad went, "Wow, Phoebe. I'll tell you what: no one else at drama stands a chance if that's how you sing on Saturday." And Sara started clapping and cheering and said, "You're *definitely* going through to the next round, Miss Franks. And Barney thinks so too."

I knew they were just being nice but I didn't care. If I could sing in front of Dad and Sara then maybe I *would* be able to sing at the auditions on Saturday.

"What did you get up to at Dad's?" Mum asked later when she came to pick us up.

"Oh, it was brilliant," squealed Sara. "You wouldn't believe it. We made popcorn and then we went into the living room and—"

"We made popcorn," I said, kicking Sara. "That's all."

The Agony of Auditions

6

"Come on, Phoebe! Dad will be here soon and your breakfast's getting cold."

I hauled myself out of bed. It was Saturday morning, the morning of the auditions, and the thought of eating breakfast made my stomach turn over. In just a few hours' time I'd actually be standing on the stage at drama auditioning for the part of Sabine.

It wasn't the best start to the day. Mum was in a state, Dad was late picking us up, and then, on the way in the car, Sara sang her own version of Sabine's song over and over, right into my ear.

"I won't be around after drama today, Phoebe, love," Dad shouted over Sara's impersonation of a dying cat. "There's something really important going on at the centre and I don't want to miss it."

I nearly said, "There's *always* something really important going on," but I didn't. I had other *more* important things to worry about and they didn't include Dad and his stupid centre!

I walked into the hall ten minutes late and everyone was already sitting in a circle.

"Sorry I'm late, Miss Howell," I mumbled, turning crimson. I know we're supposed to call Miss Howell "Mandy" at drama, but it still feels way too weird to me.

"No worries, Phoebe. I was just telling everyone that we're going to act out a few scenes from the show, practise Sabine's song, and then after break we'll start the auditions. I know it's only our second session and it's all a bit rushed but I just want to get a rough idea of who can do what."

"But we can sing with a friend, can't we?" said Ellie.

"Of course you can, Ellie. You don't have to sing by yourself – not unless you want to try out for one of the main characters, like Sabine. And don't forget what I said last week – this goes for all of you – it really doesn't matter what part you get because *everyone* in the production is important.

"Now let's go over the story before we get started. The action takes place inside this amazing factory where all our dreams are made. It's where the Sweet-Dreamers battle it out with the demon Jelly-Skulls who are responsible for giving us nightmares. The leader of the Jelly-Skulls is Gobstopper – he's a really nasty character and…"

While she carried on describing the Dream Factory I tried to work out what hope I had of getting the part of Sabine. I looked round the circle. There were thirteen girls including me.

That meant that basically I had a one in thirteen chance. Of course, *if* Miss Howell said that Sabine had to be someone with flat hair and freckles my chances would shoot up. Or, if she said that Sabine had to be someone with flat hair and freckles who could sing well, but not necessarily in front of other people, the part would practically be mine. Or, if she said that Sabine had to be someone who was...

"Now are there any questions before we start?"

"I just want to know if *I* can be Sabine or does it have to be a girl?" said Monty B, who *always* had a question. "Because you know I don't mind wearing a dress, Mandy. In the olden days, like in Shakespeare's plays, boys used to wear dresses all the time."

"I'm not quite sure what Shakespeare would've made of you in a dress, Monty B," said Miss Howell, laughing. "But I'll bear it in mind, I promise. Now I want you to grab your scripts, get into groups, and help each other practise. I'll walk round and have a good listen to each group as I go."

"Erm, Mandy, can I just say I'm really, really sorry," said Ellie, as we got up. "But we've got this new kitten, called Splat, and he *weed* all over my script. I found it this morning, dripping wet in the front room."

"Was that the script or the kitten?" said Miss Howell, handing Ellie a spare copy.

Ellie half-shrugged, looking very sheepish. "Erm...the script," she said. "But it won't happen again, I promise."

She walked to the back of the hall with Sam and I sort of trailed after them pretending to be busy with *my* script so that it didn't look as if I'd been left behind.

"What scene do you think we should do?" said Ellie, when we were sitting down. "Because I actually had a dream last night that we did a scene for the auditions but it wasn't from

The Dream Factory at all, it was from this show about giant toads, and they were…"

"*Ellie!* We haven't got time for one of your random dreams right now," said Sam. "Do you realize how important this is? Anyway, I think we should do the scene where Lolly, one of the Sweet-Dreamers, is telling Sabine and the other Sweet-Dreamers about Gobstopper's plan to get rid of Baron-Von-Bolt and Ice Bomb."

"But who *is* Gobstopper?" said Ellie. "I haven't got a clue what you're on about, you know. Is he one of the Jelly-Skulls?"

Sam shook her head. "He's like the *leader* of the Jelly-Skulls, and he's planning to take over the factory. Mandy was just telling us. Anyway, I'll be Sabine, you be Lolly, Ellie. And Phoebe, you can be Candy."

I looked at her, irritated. "But Candy hardly says anything."

Why did Sam get to decide who everyone

was going to be? She was always deciding everything. And anyway, *I* wanted to be Sabine.

We practised and practised and after a bit we could almost do the whole scene without using our scripts. But of course as soon as Miss Howell came over to see how we were getting on, I couldn't remember any of my three lines and got totally mixed up.

"Don't stress, Phoebe," she said. "It's early days yet. Even the most famous actors forget their lines sometimes."

"The toad show was so much easier." Ellie sighed. "All we had to do was croak."

We did our scene a few more times until Miss Howell said it was time for break.

"Hey, look at Polly," hissed Sam, as we grabbed our bags from the front of the stage and sat down by the piano. "Trust her!"

Polly was perched further along the edge of the stage, swinging her legs and talking to this boy called Adam. I'm not sure what school he goes to but he's older than us, thirteen I think, and *everyone* fancies him. Well, maybe not everyone, but I know Sam does, and Ellie puts on this silly, girly act every time he even looks at her, so she probably does as well.

"He goes to my school, you know," said Neesha, reading my mind. "He's in my year, and he like only thought I fancied him once, but I never did. I'm not kidding you, yeah, but my sort of best friend, Lucy – except I can't stick her any more – told *his* best friend that I wanted him to ask me out but I never did."

"You mean you actually *know* him?" said Ellie, taking some very soggy sandwiches out of her bag. "Oh look! My drink's leaked over everything."

"*Ellie!* That's minging! It's not cat wee, is it?" shrieked Neesha, grabbing her stuff away from Ellie's bag.

Ellie picked up the bag and stuck her head

inside. "No, it's definitely not wee," she said, sniffing. "But my snack's ruined."

I handed her one of my sandwiches. "I'm never going to be able to do it, you know, Ellie. I've practised loads at home, and at my dad's, but there's no way I'm going to be able to get up on that stage and sing in front of everyone."

"Stop stressing, Phoebs; you've got a brilliant voice."

"Okay, listen up, everyone," Miss Howell called out, before I could say anything else – like what's the point of having a brilliant voice if the only place you can sing is locked inside your own bedroom, or on a different planet?

"As soon as you've finished eating, I want you to make a line of chairs in front of the stage.

"Remember," she said, when we were all sitting down. "This is the song Sabine sings about all the ingredients she would need from the factory to mix her perfect dream. When you're up on the stage performing I really want to believe that you *are* Sabine – all alone without a friend in the world. I want you to make me cry!" She looked along the line. "Now who's brave enough to go first?"

Sam said she was, no surprises there, and ran round the back. She pulled the thick, metal cord and, inch by inch, almost in slow motion, the blue velvet curtains swung open and the stage stretched out behind her.

Nearly all the girls had a go even though it was obvious some of them were scared – maybe even as scared as me. I kept repeating to myself over and over, "I'll go next, Miss Howell, I'll go next, Miss Howell," but each time someone finished their turn, the words got stuck in my throat and I couldn't get them out. I felt like I was on death row or something, waiting to be executed.

When Monty B got up for his turn, he pretended to be Sabine, prancing about the stage and singing in a really high-pitched girly voice.

"What on earth are you doing, Monty B?" Miss Howell called out. "I didn't mean make me cry with *laughter*!" He did a few more dainty turns on his tip toes and then a sort of ballet leap across the stage, disappearing behind the curtain with a crash.

Next up was Catharine, and as soon as she started to sing everyone fell completely silent. Catharine is easily the prettiest *and* nicest girl in the whole group. She's in Year Eight, and not only is she totally gorgeous with these dark blue eyes and short pixie hair, but she's also got the most amazing voice. It seemed to fill the whole room and, sitting there listening to her, I knew there was no way I could get up and sing by myself.

I started to feel strange, like I was going to faint, or be sick. I tried to remember how well I'd sung round at Dad's but it was as if it had never happened. I tried to imagine standing on the stage with a great big Razzle Dazzle Smile on my face but it was hopeless. I didn't know what to do. Was I supposed to look miserable or smile? Miss Howell said *make me cry,* but I could literally *hear* Donny telling me to stick a smile on MY face. How was I supposed to get up on that great big stage – by myself – and look sad *and* smile *and* sing when I couldn't even breathe properly?

Finally, everyone who wanted to sing by themselves had had their go, except for me. "Is there *anyone* else before we get on to the acting auditions?" Miss Howell called out from the front. She looked right at me.

"Phoebe?"

And that's when I did it. I couldn't stop myself. I opened my mouth, stretched back my lips and smiled. I showed *all* my teeth – every single one – just like Donny said. I thrust my head forward and stretched my lips even further until they were practically touching my ears.

Miss Howell lurched towards me. "What's the matter, Phoebe?" she cried. "Are you feeling okay?"

"Yes!" I shouted. "I'm fine. I just want to sing. I want to be Sabine. I've dreamed about being Sabine. I know I can do it; I've got a really good voice. Give me a chance, Miss Howell, *please*."

But of course I didn't actually say anything at all – I just sat there smiling like a constipated giraffe. And suddenly I felt hot all over, which is how I always feel just before I'm about to cry.

From Bad to Worse

While Miss Howell talked about the acting auditions I slipped out of the room and into the toilets. I couldn't believe I could be so stupid. I sat down on the floor, trying not to cry; it was icy cold but I didn't care. There was no way I was going back into the hall – not after that Oscar-winning performance!

A couple of minutes later, Ellie poked her head round.

"*Phoebs*! What are you doing down there? You'll get a numb bum! It's freezing!" She sat down next to me and cuddled up. "It doesn't matter, you know; you can sing by yourself in the next show. You'll be more used to it by then. And don't forget how many times Donny got turned down before he made it."

"Don't talk to me about Donny whatever you do; I knew I should've joined karate instead of drama. You've just got no idea how much I wanted to be Sabine, Ellie. I practised that song day and night and I'm sure I must be as good as some of the others."

"Course you are, Phoebs, you're easily as good. Come on, let's go in and do our scene. I'm sure *I'm* not going to get a huge part, but remember what Mandy said about joining Star Makers; it's being part of the group that really matters."

Back in the hall Miss Howell looked over at me and smiled sympathetically, but she didn't say anything. Polly looked over and smiled as well, but it was one of her special *I'm really pleased you made an idiot of yourself* sort of smiles.

When it was time for us to do our scene, I dragged myself onto the stage. I just about managed to remember my lines – all three of them – but it was so hard with everyone else watching and I said most of my part staring down at the floor.

Sam was brilliant, of course, I knew she would be. And Ellie got the giggles halfway through, but at least she looked like she was enjoying herself. By the time it was over, my legs were like jelly and I was so relieved it was almost time to go home.

"Okay, guys," Miss Howell said, starting to pack her things away. "Tidy up the hall and then come and sit back in a circle."

I walked to the back of the room, picking up an empty water bottle and some sweet wrappers on the way. I thought about asking Miss Howell if I could sing to her after everyone had gone – I really wanted her to hear me – but I knew it was useless. I mean if I couldn't get up and sing in front of my own friends at drama, how would I ever do it in front of a load of people I'd never even met? Monty B – wearing a dress – probably had more chance of being Sabine than I did.

And then Polly came over to me.

"Oh dear, what happened, Phoebe?" she said, pretending to sound like she cared. Then she looked round at her friend, Kate, and they both burst out laughing.

I tried to think of something clever to say but my mind went totally blank. I thought about clonking her over the head with the empty water bottle I was holding, but my hand felt just as wobbly as my legs, so I walked past as quickly as I could, blinking hard to stop myself crying again.

Sitting back in a circle, Miss Howell told us that she'd give out the parts next week and that we were all superstars.

I was just wondering whether there might be a small part in the show for a non-singing, non-dancing, big-toothed giraffe when the man who rents us the hall came bursting through the door.

His name is Arthur McDermott or *"The Mad McDermott"*, as Sam calls him, and he runs his own theatre company called The Players. He's got this bushy beard that covers half his face and he wears a weird sort of black cape wrapped around his shoulders – like he's Dracula or something.

"Greetings, future stars of the stage," he said, bowing down to the ground.

"Oh, hello, Arthur," said Mandy. "How are you today?"

"Just dandy, Mandy – top of the world. And so kind of you to ask. Now the reason I've popped in is to give you a little advance warning about next week." He pulled on his beard, dislodging a few old cornflakes. "You see, I've had to arrange for some redecorating and essential maintenance work to take place in the hall, so there might be some workmen here and some...er, ladders and things. Don't worry, my dear, it won't be anything too drastic..."

He trailed off, backing towards the door.

"Well, thanks for telling me, Arthur," Miss Howell said, "but are you sure it won't be dangerous? I mean, I am working with children."

"*Dangerous?* No, no, it won't be dangerous. And anyway, you know what I always say about danger?"

"I don't actually, Arthur," muttered Miss Howell, looking pained. "But I'm sure you're going to tell me."

"I always say, *Danger? Pah! I laugh in the face of danger.*"

He threw back his head like a horse and snorted with laughter, spraying toast crumbs all over the floor. Everyone started to giggle, but I couldn't tear my eyes away from his beard – it was so disgusting. I swear if he got stranded on a desert island with nothing to eat he'd be able to feed himself for weeks.

"The thing is Mandy, it might just be a bit, well, you know... Anyway my fellow thespians,

I'm sure I can hear the telephone ringing in the office – always in demand – so I'll love you and leave you if I may."

And before Miss Howell could say anything else he spun round and escaped through the door, his black cape billowing out behind him.

"Well done for today guys," she sighed, rolling her eyes at Arthur's back as he disappeared down the corridor. "You were all stars. And don't worry if you didn't sing this time, there'll be tons more opportunities in the future."

I knew she was talking about me, and I knew she was being kind, but it just made me feel worse.

"Can you hand your scripts in. I'll give them back next week with your name and character written on the front. And bring a folder in with you, especially you, Ellie Matthews. I don't want to end up photocopying heaps more scripts because you've lost them, or the cat's weed on them! Now, are there any questions before we finish?"

"Have you decided *any* of the parts yet, Mandy?" Monty B asked. "Because I honestly don't think I can wait until next week. I mean, just imagine if I was struck down by some deadly, tropical disease and I never got to find out who I was. Oh, and Mandy, what does thespian mean?"

"It means actor, Monty," said Miss Howell, grinning. "And now it's time to say adieu, and in case you were wondering, that means goodbye."

In the car, I stared out of the window watching drips of rain run down the glass. I tried to trace them with my finger as they went from the top of the window to the bottom. Mum looked at me in the mirror.

"You're quiet, Phoebs. How did the audition go?"

"Oh, it was great. I got up and sang and I

was so good Miss Howell fainted in a heap on the floor. Okay?"

"There's no need to be sarcastic, I was only asking."

"How do you know I *was* being sarcastic?" I said. "Anyway, I don't want to talk about it – I'm too busy."

Sara poked me in the side. "How can you actually be busy sitting in the back of a car?"

"I just am. I'm busy thinking. Do you have a problem with that?"

"*Ooooh touchy!* Don't get your knickers in a knot round your big, fat bum!"

"Oh, Mum, tell her to shut up, can't you?"

"Stop bickering, both of you," Mum said. "I'm sick of you taking things out on Sara, Phoebe. It's not her fault if the audition didn't go well." She sounded tired and fed up. She always did these days.

"Anyway, you can always try again next time, can't you? It's not the end of the world.

Now what do you want for lunch? It's fish fingers or sausages."

Fish fingers? How could she talk to me about fish fingers when I'd just suffered the biggest humiliation of my life? Didn't she realize that it *was* the end of the world? Didn't she realize that my dream to be Sabine was in tatters and that I was never going to convince Miss Howell in a million years that I was the right person for the part? The next time *she* got really upset about something I'd just go on and on about lamb chops or tomato soup or something and see how she liked it.

"By the way, Phoebs, your dad said to tell you the reason he couldn't pick you up was—"

"I know, I know, he had something really important on at the centre, but what was it anyway? He never actually said when he dropped me off this morning."

"Oh, you know, just some nonsense to do with changing his name."

"To do with *what*? No wonder he never said. What's he changing it to? I bet it's something really stupid."

"I know what he's changing it to," said Sara, in her irritating, sing-song voice. "And you're right it is really stupid."

"Come on, Mum," I said. "What is it?"

"Well I think he wanted to tell you himself, Phoebs, but I don't suppose it matters if I tell you, since I've already told Sara. He's changing it to Eagle Dust, and before you ask, he did try to explain to me why but I'm afraid I stopped listening halfway through."

"Mum, you are joking, aren't you? You're not being serious. No one would change their name from something ordinary like Robert to something so...so...I can't even think of a word. I'm sorry but no one would change their name to *Eagle Dust*."

I sat back, my mind racing. What was it with my dad? Ever since he lost his job and joined

$\mathcal{L}$ife he'd gone totally loop de loop!

"You'll have to discuss it with him, Phoebe; it's something to do with this meditation course he's doing and his spiritual journey. I don't know if he's going to change it officially but it won't really affect you, will it? You'll just carry on calling him Dad."

What did she mean, it wouldn't affect me? What about when I had to introduce him to my friends, or at parents' evening? And what about when Polly Carter found out? My life would be over. And anyway, how, exactly, could having a dad called Eagle Dust *not* affect you?

Gel Spell

I was upset about the audition for days – and about Dad's ridiculous new name, but I don't think anyone even noticed. At school Polly and her friends kept sticking their necks out and grinning at me – imitating the Razzle Dazzle Smile – and then cracking up in hysterics. I really wanted to tell them to take a flying leap into the nearest lake, but I didn't have the guts.

It got so bad by the end of the week that I thought about telling Mum, but she was in the middle of some huge on-going row with Dad and I didn't want to give her even more to worry about. And I didn't really see what she could do about it anyway. It's not like she could go up to Polly and say, "Stop sticking your neck out at my daughter!" I couldn't talk it over with Ellie either, not properly, because Sam – **big mouth** – Lester was always hanging about.

On Saturday morning, I woke to the sound of the doorbell. It rang for so long it sounded as if someone was leaning against it and for a split second I thought it might actually be Polly Carter. That maybe she'd come round to get me or something. I leaped out of bed and ran to the window. But it wasn't Polly, of course it wasn't. It was some idiot with stupid tufts of red hair sticking up all over his stupid head. Monty B. Outside my house. At nine o'clock on a Saturday morning.

I stood at the window, frozen; I didn't know what to do. And then I heard voices downstairs. Mum had let him in. *Send him away*, I prayed, pulling on my jeans and a top. *Tell him I've emigrated, or fallen down a hole. Anything.*

I glanced in the mirror. I looked terrible. My

hair was even worse than usual, stuck to the sides of my head like two slices of wet ham. I was supposed to be changing my image this morning. I had it all planned. I'd read the rest of Donny's article – the section about hair gel – and Donny swore that using gel had transformed his life beyond all recognition. **Gel Spell**, he called it. **Think Smooth! Think Shine! Think Hot!**

Sad, I know, but I was desperate, and unlike the **Razzle Dazzle Smile**, which took years to perfect, **Gel Spell** was instant. I knew it was too late to get the part of Sabine but it had to be worth a go! I sort of figured that if I looked totally different, no one would remember my Great Giraffe Impersonation at the auditions. I'd bought some gel in the week – **fast drying, extra-firm hold hair glosser** it said on the jar – but now I'd overslept and Monty B had turned up and there was no time to sort it out.

"Phoebe, come down for breakfast," Mum

called out. "Monty B's here for you. Or do you want me to send him up?"

"No! I'm not ready," I squealed, grabbing the pot of hair gel and slapping a load onto my head. The second I did it I knew it was a mistake – it was wet and slimy and there was way too much of it. I tried to spread it about but it started to run down the sides of my face like it was alive, and it seemed to be growing. I grabbed some tissues to try and wipe it off, but the more I smoothed it back the worse it got. It was everywhere. Soggy bits of blue tissue were coming off in my hair; tiny scraps of it, stuck on like a collage. All I needed was a sprinkle of glitter and I'd look like something Sara used to bring home from nursery.

Suddenly there was a bang on the door. I jumped up and let out a small scream. Sara flew into the room and then stopped dead. *"Oh my God, Phoebe! What have you done?"* she whispered, looking scared. "Oh, and Mum said to tell you that breakfast's ready and your boyfriend's gone."

She flew back out of the room before I could thump her. I could hear her snorting all the way down the stairs as I gave my hair one last frantic wipe and traipsed down behind her for breakfast.

"Monty B was here," said Mum as I walked in to the kitchen. "He wanted to give you a lift up to drama but I said you'd see him up there. I didn't know you two were such good friends."

"We're not," I said, drying my slimy hands on the nearest tea towel. "He just thinks everything's the same as it used to be when he lived next door, but it isn't."

"Can I use your bike today while you're at drama?" Sara asked suddenly.

"Don't be stupid, it's way too big for you. Your feet don't even touch the ground."

"But couldn't I just try? I've grown at least three milli-inches in the last few months."

"Three *what*? Oh, okay then. Whatever."

Mum looked at me sharply as if she couldn't believe what she was hearing. She hadn't even noticed my hair but she'd noticed me being nice to Sara quick enough.

"That hair gel must've rotted your brain or something," said Sara. "You *never* let me use your things."

"She's just preoccupied with drama, aren't you, Phoebs? Isn't today the day you find out your parts?"

"Yeah, but I'm not that bothered because I know I'm going to be one of the Sweet-Dreamers so it's no big deal."

Of course it *was* a big deal really – the biggest. But I wasn't about to tell Mum that I was still hoping against hope, that somehow, by some miracle, Miss Howell would choose me to be Sabine.

"I could read the tea leaves and tell you for sure, if you want?" Sara said, picking up Mum's empty cup and throwing a tea towel over her head.

"She doesn't use tea leaves, *raisin brain*, she uses tea bags."

"Well anyway, I've read the whole script, and Miss Howell would definitely choose *me* to be Sabine if she ever heard me sing."

"More like she'd run away screaming! And keep your hands off my stuff."

Sara stuck her tongue out at me. "You're just jealous," she said, and crammed a huge piece of toast into her mouth.

Mum reached out and touched my forehead.

"Are you sure you're okay, Phoebe? You're ever so pale and you haven't eaten properly for days."

"I'm fine, Mum, honest. I'll just go and get my stuff together. Dad will be here in a sec."

I raced upstairs to see if I could do anything with my hair – but before I could even start to sort it out Dad arrived and we had to leave.

Walking up the road to the car we bumped in to Mrs. Burton and her three-year-old Brain of Britain grandson, Jason.

"Lovely day for an outing," she trilled, even though it was freezing cold and about to pour.

"Oh, hello, Valerie," said Dad.

"We're off to the Science Museum," she said, as if we cared. "Jason just *loves* museums. We've been taking him to museums ever since he was a baby. Never too young to educate them, that's what we always say. He was practically reading by the time he was one, you know."

She raised her eyebrows and started to nod, and Dad started to nod back as if someone else was controlling his head. He didn't say anything; he just stood there nodding like he was in a trance or something. In the end I had to pull him towards the car or else he'd probably still be there, standing in the middle of the street, nodding.

When we arrived, Ellie and Sam were standing outside waiting for me, hopping up and down in the cold. Sam grabbed my arm and pulled me towards the door.

"Come *on*, Phoebe, we've been standing out here for ages and we're dying to find out our parts."

"Don't exaggerate, Sam, we only got here five minutes ago," said Ellie, giving me a quick hug. "Oh, what happened to your hair, Phoebs? Didn't you have time to dry it?"

Upstairs I could just about make out Miss Howell through the thick, choking dust. She was standing in the middle of the hall surrounded by ladders, toolboxes and open pots of paint – and she looked furious. The walls were brilliant turquoise, with huge, brightly coloured tropical fish painted on top. All the windows had been left open so it was freezing, but even with the windows open the smell was so strong it was difficult to breathe and my eyes started to water.

"I actually don't believe this," Miss Howell was muttering to herself. "I'll give him, *laugh in the face of danger!* We can't rehearse under these conditions. It's not safe for a start and it stinks. I'm not putting up with this. I mean I'm sorry, Mr. Arthur McDermott, but I do pay to hire this hall!"

She stormed out of the room and down the corridor to Arthur's office, but it wasn't as if he was going to be sitting there waiting for her. Anyway, I was far more worried about the state of my hair than the state of the hall. It felt disgusting, and I was sure everyone was staring at me.

I stood over to one side by myself and made out I was incredibly interested in a bright yellow and pink painted fish, while I tried to pick out as many bits of blue tissue as I could. Ellie called out to me a few times but I pretended I couldn't hear. Then Monty B came over.

"Hi, Frankie," he said. "Like the hair! Shame you weren't ready this morning but it was great to see your mum and Sara after so long. I suppose your dad was still in bed – having a lie-in."

"He doesn't live at home any more," I mumbled, my face burning up. I don't even know why I said it. There was just something about the way he came out with stuff, like we were still neighbours and nothing had changed.

"Bummer," he said. "Because last time I saw him, before *we* moved out, he said I could borrow his guitar."

"*What?*" I couldn't believe he was for real. "Do you mean you came round to my house at nine o'clock on a Saturday morning because *two years ago* my dad said you could borrow his guitar?" I wanted to grab hold of him and shake him. He was *so* annoying.

"Well it was a pretty cool guitar," he said.

"But that's not the real reason I came over."

Miss Howell stormed back into the hall before I could ask him what he was on about. She looked around the room, frowning.

"Right, listen up, guys; we'll have to start the session on the stage. It's not ideal, I know, but it's the best we can do at the moment."

"Oh my God," said Neesha, holding her nose. "Did you find Arthur, because I swear it's minging in here?"

"No, of course I didn't find him," Miss Howell said, running her hand through her hair. "You didn't think he was going to stick around after leaving the hall like this, did you, Neesha? He's probably in Timbuktu or somewhere by now!"

Up on the stage, we all sat in a circle. Miss Howell took a big piece of paper out of her bag with CAST written at the top and everyone stopped talking.

"Quick, Mandy, put me out of my misery,"

Monty B groaned. "Be honest, I can take it. Am I Sabine or not?"

"Er...not, Monty B," she said, laughing. "But I'm glad you asked because I was just about to say that I really hope you'll *all* be happy with your parts. Remember what I said before the auditions – *everyone* in a production is important no matter how big or small your part is."

My tummy lurched over suddenly, like when you go on a really scary ride at the fair and I stared down at the floor.

"Okay, let's get started. Catharine – you're going to be Sabine," said Miss Howell, smiling at Catharine. "Well done."

Catharine looked thrilled and everyone gave her a clap. I knew she deserved it because she's a brilliant singer and it was obvious *I* wasn't going to be Sabine, but still I couldn't help feeling gutted.

"This is *amazing*," said Catharine, her eyes

106

shining so brightly it looked like she was about to cry. "I really, *really* wanted to be Sabine but I didn't think I was going to get it."

"Well, I *did* want to be Sabine to start with," said Sam, tossing her blonde curls. "But then I changed my mind because it's not actually the biggest part, is it?"

"Not as big as your head," said Monty B, and I nearly burst out laughing.

Sam made a face at Monty B and Miss Howell finished reading through the rest of the cast list, explaining that anyone who didn't have a main part was going to be either a Sweet-Dreamer or a Jelly-Skull.

"I've written the name of your character on the top of your scripts so you'll see who you are in a sec when I hand them out."

She passed round the scripts and everyone started to talk at once.

"I can't believe I'm Gobstopper. I'd better get used to acting really nasty!"

"I've got to text my mum! She knew how much I wanted to be Fizz-Wiz."

"But Mandy, does this mean I don't get to wear a dress?"

"Look, Adam, we're doing a song together!"

"This is going to be so wicked!"

I looked around the circle. Everyone seemed to be pretty happy with their parts. My script had "Lolly" written at the top and I quickly flicked through to see how many lines I had. I knew Lolly was the youngest and smallest of all the Sweet-Dreamers, and that at the end of the show she helps Sabine to escape from the Dream Factory.

"Hey, guess what, Frankie? I'm Sherbet, one of the Sweet-Dreamers," said Monty B, plonking himself down next to me and shoving his script in my face. "But don't worry; I *do* get to wear a dress because I've got an extra part in one of the main songs in Act Two. How about you? If you're a Sweet-Dreamer, and we're like in the same scenes, you could come over to mine to practise."

I carried on looking through my lines, ignoring Monty B. As if I was going to go over to his! I wanted him to move away from me anyway so he wouldn't notice that my hair was full of shredded, blue tissue. I'd almost got to the end of the script, and was just about to close it, when I spotted something that made me stop dead. On the very last page, right at the very end of the show, there was a short song and it was sung by Lolly...*alone!*

Cement Head!

"Erm...Miss Howell," I said, pointing at Lolly's solo in the script. "This must be a mistake, isn't it?"

"No, Phoebe, of course it's not a mistake. At the end of the play Lolly is very upset because she's worried Sabine will forget her when she leaves the Dream Factory, and this is the song she sings about how much she's going to miss her."

"But *you* said that anyone who wanted a solo singing part *had* to sing by themselves at the auditions, and I never did! Remember? I didn't sing at all. And anyway, I can't sing by myself, you know I can't. I'll never be able to do it. Not ever. Not in a million years. I'll just ruin the whole show, I'll...I'll..."

I was so panicked by now I felt like bashing Miss Howell on the head with my script to make her realize what a terrible, awful, catastrophic mistake she'd made. I mean, *me* – Phoebe Franks – *sing a solo?*

"Of course you won't ruin the show, Phoebe. I wouldn't have given the part to you if I didn't think you could do it. I've heard you sing with the rest of the group – you're going to be awesome. And it *is* only five lines. You'll be fine, trust me."

She turned back to the rest of the group. "Right, let's start reading through. The show opens with Sabine in the factory. She's sitting there dreaming about the life she wishes she could lead when Lolly wakes up crying because she's had a nightmare."

She's had a nightmare? What about me? This was like the worst nightmare ever. It might be *only five lines* to Miss Howell, but to me it was like trying to climb a mountain blindfolded and with my legs tied together – only harder. There was no way I'd ever be able to do it. There was actually more chance of Polly Carter walking right up to me in front of everyone at drama and announcing that she wanted me to be her best friend. In fact...

Monty B nudged me. "Wake up, Frankie, it's your line."

The rest of the session passed in a blur of fear and dust and at break time Miss Howell went back out to look for Arthur.

"Hey, Phoebe, groovy hairstyle," Catharine said. She sat down next to me and unwrapped her sandwiches. "Seriously, it really suits you pushed back off your face like that."

I touched my hair; it was rock hard like a lump of cement.

"You've got a great part, too, aren't you pleased?"

"Yeah, I suppose," I mumbled. "Except that

I've got to sing by myself, which is like the biggest joke."

"No, it isn't, you'll be wicked."

Neesha came over and helped herself to some of Catharine's crisps. "I thought for sure I was gonna be Gobstopper but I'm one of the other Jelly-Skulls," she said, stuffing the crisps in her mouth. "And, oh my God, yeah, have I ever told you about the time when I was actually eating a Gobstopper and I was talking really fast, and I breathed in at the wrong moment and the Gobstopper—"

Just then Ellie burst in to the hall. "Mandy's really upset!" she cried, interrupting Neesha. "She's out in the corridor on the phone to Arthur, and she said that if he doesn't get the hall sorted by next week we won't be rehearsing here any more."

"She's just bluffing," said Sam. "Anyway, never mind about the hall, I've got a far more serious problem than that. I'm Ice Bomb, the

President's wife, which is like the best part, but it means I've got to be married to *Adam*!"

She pulled a face as if it was the most awful thing in the world but I knew she was putting it on. She was crazy about Adam.

"There will be no pulling faces in *my* factory!" Adam called over, grinning at Sam. "No pulling faces, no laughing, no smiling, no talking, no burping and definitely no breathing."

As he was talking, Monty B crept up behind him and burped right into his ear and then for some reason he turned round and burped into mine.

"Urrghh! That is *so* disgusting," Polly Carter shrieked. She leaned over and whispered something to some of the other girls, probably something about how stupid my hair looked, and they cracked up.

"Don't worry, Frankie," Monty B called over his shoulder. "I promise I won't burp when we do our kissing scene."

I looked at him, horrified. I could feel my face start to burn up. Why was he always doing that? Calling me Frankie and talking to me in front of the others as if we were best friends or something?

"Oh my God, I'm not kidding you, yeah, but I so pity anyone who's got a kissing scene with you, Monty B," said Neesha, and Polly and her cronies practically fell off the stage laughing.

We spent the rest of the session reading through the script and learning one of the main songs in the show, *Scream!* Arthur never turned up at all, Tara Perkins had to go home early because the dust had made her wheezy, and it was actually a huge relief at one o'clock to get out into the fresh air.

"Why don't you come over to mine, Phoebs?" said Ellie, rolling up her script and using it as a telescope to try and spot her mum. "Sam's coming and my mum said you can both stay for tea."

"Okay. I'll just ask my dad, hang on a sec."

Dad seemed a bit upset. He mumbled something about how he never gets to see me any more, and how he had something important to ask me, but that if I *really* wanted to go it was okay, he'd tell me later. I could've pointed out that he never seems all that bothered about seeing me when he's got something important on at the centre, like renaming himself for instance, but I just jumped into the car with Ellie and Sam before he could change his mind.

"I know what we could do when we get back to yours, Ellie," said Sam. "Let's start making up a dance to *Don't Let the Bed-Bugs Bite* and then show it to Mandy next week."

"Oh yeah, I love that one," said Ellie, peeling a banana and then stuffing a huge piece into her mouth. "It's like my favourite song in the whole show."

Sam screwed up her face. "Oh *gross*, Ellie!

I can see your banana all mushed up in your mouth, it's disgusting! And we didn't understand a word you said, did we, Phoebs? It sounded like, 'Itshnnnnn iknnnn mhhhhhy...'"

"Shut up! No, it didn't!"

We all started to laugh and for the first time in ages I began to feel happy.

Back at Ellie's we moved everything round so that there was space to dance. Her room is tiny and it's always a complete tip, but if the bed is pushed right up against the wall and the chest-of-drawers goes sideways, we can make quite a good area in the middle.

"Right, Phoebe, you stand here because you're the shortest," said Sam, placing me in between her and Ellie. "Ellie, you sing, *It's the middle of the night, keep your eyes closed tight*, I'll sing, *You try to fall asleep with all of your might*, and Phoebs, you sing, *But don't let the bed-bugs bite*. Then we'll *all* sing, *I said, don't let the bed-bugs bite*."

We put on the music and tried it out a few times and it worked really well so we started to make up a dance to go with it. I knew Sam was being bossy but for once I didn't care. It was so nice to be singing and dancing and mucking about and not thinking about all the stuff that was getting me down that I couldn't believe it when Ellie's mum came in with sandwiches and drinks and said it was four-thirty.

I grabbed a carton of juice and collapsed on the bed. "What do you think about the parts then?"

"Mine's brilliant," said Sam. "Ice Bomb is easily the best part in the show *and* I get to do loads of scenes with Adam."

"You know, I still don't really get the whole story," said Ellie, doing a backbend in the middle of the room.

"What do you mean, you still don't get the whole story?" cried Sam, sitting on top of her and squashing her down to the floor.

"Ooof! Get off, you great lump, I can't breathe!"

"*Just listen a minute Ellie; it's important!* Baron-Von-Bolt and Ice Bomb run the Dream Factory, and they've got loads of money, right? But they're horribly mean and greedy and they treat their workers really badly. So anyway, Gobstopper decides he's going to get rid of Baron-Von-Bolt and Ice Bomb and run the factory himself, only he's really evil as well. But then Lolly – that's *Phoebe* – finds out what he's planning and saves the day."

"Oh, so that means you end up the hero of the show, Phoebe," said Ellie, from somewhere underneath Sam.

"Yeah," said Sam. "Like, from zero to hero!"

"What about Polly?" I said, ignoring Sam. "She'll be great as Gobstopper, won't she? She's exactly like him already."

I was dying to tell Ellie about Polly, but not while Sam was there.

"Perfect casting!" said Sam. "I heard her say something really mean about you, today, Phoebe. Something about how quiet you were reading out your lines and that if you were that quiet sitting in a circle, who'd ever hear you in a theatre with an audience?"

Ellie sat up, looking cross. "Well, I could hear *all* your lines, Phoebs, and I was sitting a long way away. Hey, have I shown you my new top? I got it as a sort of early Christmas present from my auntie."

She jumped up and rummaged around in a pile of clothes that looked as if they'd been there for years and from somewhere near the bottom she pulled out a gorgeous pink top with purple sleeves and collar.

Sam grabbed it and pulled it on over her T-shirt. "Where did she get this? I *love* it!"

"Careful, Sam, don't stretch it! And look, I got matching nail varnish."

"D'ya know what, Phoebe?" said Sam, as

she pulled the top back over her head and dropped it on the pile of clothes. "I swear someone at drama fancies you, but you'll never guess who it is, not in a billion years."

"Don't be stupid," I said, blushing. "No one fancies me."

"No, I'm dead serious," she said. "It must be your new hairstyle – *the sleeked-back look*. I noticed him staring at you today, like *all* the time. Okay, I'll give you a clue. His name begins with M and he's quite fit, in a weird sort of way, but don't worry it's not The Mad McDermott. Come on, take a guess."

"It's not Monty B, is it?" said Ellie.

"Shut up," I said, trying to run my hands through my hair. It wouldn't surprise me if Monty B *was* staring at me. He was probably wondering why I had a massive lump of cement instead of a head.

"I can't bear Monty B," I said. "He's such an idiot. He burped right in my ear at break time."

"But that's because he loves you!" shrieked Sam. And they both collapsed back on the bed, clutching hold of each other in hysterics.

As soon as I got home I locked myself in the bathroom and washed all the gel and tissue out of my hair. If I was going to transform myself it was pretty clear I was going to have to do it without Donny's help. He might be able to work his magic with a flashy smile and a load of hair gel, but it obviously wasn't going to work for me.

10

Dad's
Great idea...

"So come on then, who are you?" Mum said, the next morning at breakfast. "I meant to ask you yesterday when you got back from Ellie's."

"I'm just Lolly – one of the Sweet-Dreamers. I told you I would be. Ellie's a Sweet-Dreamer as well, she's Fizz-Wiz, but Sam got one of the biggest parts, she's Ice Bomb."

"What exactly is a Sweet-Dreamer?"

"Oh, they make everyone's *sweet* dreams," said Sara, butting in. "But then there are the Jelly-Skulls, yeah? They turn the sweet dreams into—"

I put my hand over her mouth. Whose show was it, for goodness' sake? "Anyway I've got to sing a solo, which is like the biggest joke, so I don't even know if I'm going to carry on."

"Talking about big jokes," mumbled Sara, sinking her teeth into my hand. "The biggest joke is you putting gel on your hair to impress your boyfriend. And don't deny it because you know it's true."

She was going to have to go, my little sister – and quick!

I spent most of the day up in my room trying to learn my lines, but it was really difficult to concentrate. Every time I thought about singing my solo, my palms got sweaty, and the words on the script started to swim about in front of my eyes. It's like part of me was thinking I *would* be able do it and everything would be fine, but part of me was convinced I'd collapse in heap or die if I even *tried* to sing in front of the others.

If only I was more like my character, Lolly, I'd have the guts to sing my solo *and* stand up to Polly Carter. Lolly's easily the bravest Sweet-Dreamer in the whole show. Even though she's dead scared of Gobstopper, she finds out what he's up to, reports him to the dream-police and helps Sabine escape from the factory. Just imagine if there really was such a thing as the dream-police, it would be brilliant. I'd be able to phone them up, report Polly for bullying, and get rid of her for good.

On Wednesday when I came out of school, Dad was there to meet me. He was wearing a white T-shirt with $\mathcal{L}i\!fe$ written across the front, the oldest, scruffiest pair of jeans I've ever seen and his awful brown sandals. He looked as if he'd just come back from a music festival or something. I tried to get him away as fast as I could before anyone else came out and saw him.

"I'm pleased I caught you, Phoebe," he said. "I missed you on Saturday and there was something I wanted to talk to you about."

I turned round to make sure no one was coming up behind us, but the coast was clear.

"How was school?" he asked, as we started to walk home.

"Okay, I guess. What did you want to talk about?" I wondered if it was something to do with Mum, or if he'd finally managed to get a new job.

"Well you know how Miss Howell has been asking parents to come in and talk about their professions or hobbies to the class, erm...if they're unusual or a bit different? Well...I've been thinking it might..."

I stopped dead and looked at him in horror. "Oh no, Dad, please don't say what I think you're going to say."

"It's just I thought it might be nice if I came in to your class and gave a talk about the $\mathcal{L}ife$ centre and the sorts of things we do there."

"But Dad!" I grabbed his arm. "You can't. I'll die! Don't you care about me at all? You can't come in to my class and talk about spiritual journeys and stuff like that. I mean you only joined the stupid group so that you wouldn't have to spend any time with me on Saturdays."

Dad swung me round to face him. He looked really upset, but I didn't care. "Come on, Phoebe, you know that's not true. You mean everything to me, you and Sara."

"But Dad!"

My hands were trembling. I wanted to grab hold of him and shake him hard till he realized what a nightmare this was.

The whole *Life* thing started when we went on holiday to Cornwall, a few months after Dad lost his job. We were down at the beach on the first day and Dad got talking to this man called Spirit who was out walking his dog. Spirit was a member of *Life* and he told my dad that if he learned how to look *inwards* or something then he'd be able to transform *his* life. They ended up in the pub, sitting there for hours talking and drinking coffee, their heads bent close together. I remember Mum kept trying to get Dad to come back down to the beach and spend some time with us, but he didn't want to.

On the last day of the holiday I found this incredible shell. It was really smooth and it had a sort of shiny, rainbow-coloured fossil embedded in it. Before I went to bed that night I left the shell on my dad's pillow but I don't think he even noticed it. When I went into their room the next morning it was shoved under the bed and he never said thank you or mentioned it or anything. It was as if he could only see Spirit and the rest of us had become invisible.

As soon as we got back from the holiday Dad joined a $\mathcal{L}$ife centre near us and bit by bit he started to change. He began to wear different clothes for a start – tie-dyed T-shirts and those horrid, brown sandals, and then a few months after that he became a vegetarian. He even tried to get rid of the TV because according to him it was "quenching our creativity".

Then one morning he came into the kitchen while Mum was making us breakfast and said, "Maxine, my love, I can see your aura and it's very dull. Please, Max, you need to let go of your negativity. Just take a deep breath and watch it float away."

Mum, who was holding an empty saucepan at the time, took a *really* deep breath, bashed the saucepan on his head *really* hard and stormed out of the room.

A few days later, well nineteen to be precise, they broke up. He moved in to his flat on the other side of town and that was the end of that. I've still got the shell though, from the holiday. I sleep with it under my pillow every night.

I looked at Dad now. He was staring down at the pavement and I could see this little talk wasn't going the way he thought it would.

"What are you going to say anyway?" I muttered. "'Hi, everyone. My name is Eagle Dust and I'm on a journey?' I'm not going in that day; I swear I'm not. And you can't make me."

"Come on, Phoebe, it's not that bad is it? It might be quite interesting. I could talk to your class about meditating and about how everyone is surrounded by their own special aura." He started to get excited; his voice growing louder by the second. "I could even talk to them about past-life experiences and hands-on healing."

Hands-on what? Sometimes I wondered if aliens didn't come down to Earth one day and beam my pretty ordinary sort of a dad up into their spaceship to reprogram his brain. Maybe he was just part of some weird outer-space experiment.

Suddenly I heard sniggering from behind us. I whipped round and there was Polly Carter with her stupid friends gazing at Dad as if he did come from a different planet and I could feel myself start to burn up. I pulled Dad away from them and we walked home in silence. What would I say anyway? *Thanks for humiliating me in front of my arch-enemy – good one, Dad.* I was so angry I could feel my hands itching to punch him.

"You know, you shouldn't care what everyone else thinks, Phoebs," he said suddenly, as if he could see right inside my head.

"That's easy for you to say," I whispered, clenching and unclenching my fists. "And anyway, why did you join your stupid group in the first place?"

Dad didn't say anything for ages. I wasn't even sure he'd heard me or that I'd actually said it out loud. But then halfway down our road, he stopped walking and turned me to face him again, bending down so that our faces were practically touching. I squirmed away, embarrassed. I didn't know what he was going to say but whatever it was I didn't want to hear it. My stomach was in knots and I wished I'd kept my mouth shut.

He pulled me back towards him and I could feel his hands digging into my arms.

"I *had* to join the group, Phoebs," he said. "I *had* to join because the centre was the only place where I didn't feel I was going mad; the only place where I could make sense of things. The $\mathcal{Life}$ group literally saved *my* life."

I didn't know what he was on about. When I was younger he used to say *we* were his life, me and Sara; that he couldn't live without *us* – but as soon as he started going to the centre it was like we didn't even matter any more.

"Look, Phoebe, I know it's difficult for you to understand at your age but when I lost my job at the nursery it was like something inside me died. That job was part of me. It was who I was. When they took it away I didn't know what I was going to do. Your mum didn't understand – she thought I could just go out and get another job in a factory or a shop, but it wasn't as simple as that; my work at the nursery was special. When I turned up for interviews, dressed in a suit, trying to be something I wasn't, I didn't feel right. I felt like a fish out of water. Do you know what I mean?"

I nodded. I did know what he meant. It was just how I'd felt ever since I started at Woodville. Like a fish out of water. I wanted to go back to my old pond at Merryhill Primary more than anything.

"Do you think you'll ever come home?" I said, tears pricking at the corners of my eyes.

He stared at me for the longest time. He looked so sad and I knew what he was going to say.

"Do you?" I whispered.

He shook his head.

I yanked my arms away from him and tore down the road, straight past Mrs. Bolton who gave me one of her stupid interfering looks. I banged on the front door over and over until my hands hurt and when Mum let me in I pushed past her and ran upstairs to my room.

A Little Miracle
11

I felt awful the next morning; about Dad *and* about Polly Carter and her manky mates overhearing him outside school. Dad actually called to say he wouldn't come in and talk to my class after all – not if it was going to upset me, and even though I was relieved I couldn't help feeling bad, like I should've had the guts to stand up to Polly Carter – and not feel so ashamed of my own dad.

The week dragged by. I learned my lines and practised my solo and tried my best to stay out of Polly's way. Eating breakfast the following Saturday, I thought about all the things I *could've* said when I saw them standing there like that, sniggering and pointing. I bet

Neesha would've thought of something in a second if someone was laughing at *her* dad. She's always got something quick and funny to say – but my brain just doesn't seem to work that fast. Maybe I could get her to give me some special, *Put Down Polly Carter* lessons or something?

"What on earth are you thinking about, Phoebe?" said Mum. "You've been staring at that bacon roll for ages with a very strange expression on your face. Hurry up and finish, will you, I want you by the front door and ready to go to drama when your dad gets here. Oh, and Gran's coming over later so tell him he needs to bring you straight home."

I wanted to say, "Tell him yourself," but Mum and Dad were barely speaking these days.

Walking up the stairs into the hall, Polly was just ahead of me when she called out over her shoulder, "I hear your dad's going to buy you your own special aura for Christmas, Phoebe," and then burst out laughing, clutching hold of the banister as if she was in danger of falling down. I could feel myself shrivel up inside as I tried to think of something to say back, *anything*, but just then Tara came over and grabbed my arm.

"Thank goodness you're here, Phoebe!" she cried, pulling me into the hall. "You've got to test me on Act One – I've been practising all week but for some reason I still seem to be getting my lines mixed up."

I don't think she was getting her lines mixed up – I mean she's easily the cleverest girl in our class – she was probably just trying to get me away from Polly before I pushed her back down the stairs or something.

"Hi, Phoebe," said Ellie, coming over and giving me a hug. "What do you think of the hall? It's wicked, isn't it? It's like standing in the middle of a giant aquarium. Sam and I are going Christmas shopping later if you want to come. My mum's going to drop us at the High Road after drama."

"I can't Ellie. My gran's coming over and I have to go straight home."

Just then Miss Howell walked over to us. "Look at the state of the hall, girls! I honestly don't know what goes on in that man's head. I mean, doesn't he realize that fluorescent turquoise doesn't exactly match sunset orange?"

She touched her hair, which was the brightest orange I've ever seen and actually much more like a tangerine than a sunset. I'd put *my* hair up in a sort of knot with bits hanging down. I copied it from this magazine. It probably didn't look anything like the girl in the picture, but at least it wasn't plastered with hair gel and bits of blue tissue.

"Anyway, come and make a circle over here and we'll get started, and Ellie, don't even tell me you've lost your script or its been weed on again because I don't want to know."

"I haven't actually *lost* it," said Ellie, shrugging sheepishly. "I just dropped it in the bath and then it was drying over the radiator, but I think my little brother might have taken it and used it to...er...line the hamster cage."

"*The hamster cage!*" said Miss Howell, trying not to laugh. "Ellie Matthews, what am I going to do with you? Anyway, you won't need it this morning because in a second we're going to learn some exercises to help you project your voices when you're onstage. At the moment most of you are speaking and singing from up here at the top of your chest, when your voice actually needs to come from way down here in your belly.

"Let's start off by going round the circle and each of you saying your name as loudly as you can without shouting. I want you to put one hand on your tummy, then when you speak you should feel it go right in."

"My tummy's not moving at all," said Monty B. "But that's probably because I had six bowls of cornflakes for breakfast."

"Oh my God, that is so gross," said Neesha.

I hate it when we have to say things out loud in front of everyone else; I'd actually rather have a hole drilled in one of my teeth with no anaesthetic. I tried to tell Miss Howell I didn't want to do it, but she just said I'd be fine. By the time it got to my turn in the circle, my heart was thumping so loud in my chest I had no idea whether my voice was coming from the bottom of my belly or the top of my big toe.

"Not bad at all," Miss Howell said when we'd all had a go. "But now I want you to spend about five minutes or so talking to the person sitting next to you. Then when you're ready, you're going to stand on the stage with your partner, introduce them to the rest of the group, and tell me one interesting fact about them.

I'm going to stand at the back of the hall and if I can hear you, I'll wave."

Ellie was sitting on my right, but she was already talking to Sam, who was sitting next to her on the other side. Sitting to my left was Polly Carter. Great!

"Come on then, Phoebe," she said, giving me one of her nastiest smiles. "Tell me something interesting – like how's your dad this week?"

"Very funny, Polly! How's *yours*?"

"Shut up!"

We both sat there in silence for a minute while everyone around us chatted away. I couldn't think of anything to say because what I really wanted to say was, "Why are you always such a witch to me?" But then suddenly Polly put her head down and I realized she was crying.

"Hey, listen, Polly, I'm sorry. I didn't mean—"

She lifted her head again and wiped her eyes angrily.

"Forget it. I'm fine," she said, her voice stone hard. She sat there for a bit staring into the distance. "And don't tell anyone I was crying because I wasn't, *okay?*"

"Okay. I wasn't going to tell anyone anyway. But are you all right?"

"I'm fine – I just said so didn't I? Look, why don't you just tell everyone that my dad's new girlfriend is going to have a baby and that I'm going to have a half-brother? *That's an interesting fact isn't it?*"

I looked at her, amazed. I didn't even know that her mum and dad had split up, or that her dad was with someone else.

"Are you sure that's what you want me to say?"

She didn't answer me. She just stared straight ahead again, her body rigid.

"Well, you can tell everyone that *my* dad's

142

changing his name at a special ceremony if you want," I said. "But I can't tell you what he's changing it to – it's way too embarrassing."

She still didn't say anything, but she sort of smiled and her eyes didn't look quite so mean. Her family seemed to be in an even bigger mess than mine – maybe that's why she was so horrible. But I still didn't get why she picked on *me* all the time – and I still didn't know what I was supposed to do about it.

By the time it got round to our turn to speak I was so distracted by what Polly had said about her dad, I totally forgot to be nervous, and when I'd finished introducing her and telling everyone that she was going to have a half-brother, I realized that Miss Howell was waving madly at me from the end of the hall.

"That was fantastic, Phoebe Franks!" she shouted. "Never mind about back here – they probably heard that in the next town.

 143

And congratulations Polly! A new baby – how exciting!"

"This is Phoebe," said Polly when she introduced me. "Her dad is changing his name, but I'm not going to tell you what he's changing it to because it's top, *top* secret!" She made it sound dead exciting like Dad was involved in some sort of dangerous, underground mission and no one laughed or anything.

I couldn't believe it. The whole thing was like a miracle. I'd spoken out loud in front of everyone in the group without wetting myself or collapsing in a heap. And my arch-enemy, Polly Carter, had turned into a normal human being. Well, for a couple of seconds anyway. I turned round to say thanks but she'd walked over to the other side of the hall and she had her back to me.

Next up were Monty B and Adam. Monty B bounced onto the stage grinning like a madman, and introduced Adam. Then he started to talk and it was obvious that he had no intentions of stopping.

"This is Adam. He goes to Fern Bay Secondary and he's in Year Nine. He loves coming to drama but his favourite subject at school is art and he once won a big competition so it's like he's already famous in a way.

"I'm definitely going to be famous when I'm older," he went on, hopping about from one foot to the other. "I'll probably be an actor or a comedian or something. I've got some great jokes I could tell you, like there's this one about two boiled eggs but it's really long so...anyway, Adam's got two brothers and one sister and he's the youngest. You know I used to be the youngest in my family as well, Mandy, and it – was – the – pits. Then my younger brother was born, which was great, except that now I'm a middle child and *everyone* knows that middle children—"

"Monty B!" Miss Howell called out. "I said

one interesting fact, not his entire life story with a bit of yours thrown in for good measure!"

"But Mandy—"

"Stop! Stop! Cut! ENOUGH!"

"Okay, I get the message. NO NEED TO PROJECT YOUR VOICE LIKE THAT!" he shouted, and stormed off the stage pretending to be in a huff.

In the break, Polly stayed on the other side of the room with two of her friends. I tried to catch her eye a few times and smile at her, but she was back to sneering and laughing.

After break we stood round the piano and practised *Doing the Sweet-Dream Rap* and *Don't Let the Bed-Bugs Bite*. It was amazing how much better we sang after doing those exercises. It felt as if the sound was filling the whole room, and none of us noticed Arthur walk in until the song we were singing came to an end.

"Voices of angels," he said, making us all jump. "Look at me, Mandy, I'm tingling all over."

"Oh, hello, Arthur, I didn't see you there," said Miss Howell, getting up from the piano. "Hall's looking lovely and er...turquoise."

"Yes, stunning, isn't it? Splendid, in fact... just the ticket."

"Just the ticket for what, exactly?" Miss Howell muttered.

"All will be revealed in good time, Mandy. All in good time."

"Look, why don't you just tell me now, Arthur, since you're here. Put me out of my misery."

Arthur clasped his hands together like he was praying. "But Mandy, my dear, the secret of a good friendship is trust. And a friendship without trust is like an actor without a stage. I forget who said that, but it's beautiful, isn't it?"

 147

I looked over at Mandy. Her fist was clenched tight and I was sure she was about to swing it at Arthur. She took a very deep breath.

"There was one thing," he went on. "Trouble is, that lovely singing has knocked it right out of my head. Something to do with next week... now what was it?"

He pulled hard on his beard, and a big bit of croissant floated down to the ground.

"No, it's gone...oh well, it'll come to me... carry on...voices like angels...I'll pop back when I remember...toodle pip for now."

He gave a theatrical bow and with a quick flick of his cape he legged it out of the room. Of course he didn't come back, and Miss Howell ended the session by suggesting we hold a competition to see who could guess what *was* going to happen the following week.

A Christmas Wish...

It was about half-past three and just starting to get dark when Gran arrived.

"Get the kettle on," she called out from the car, just like she always does – and I ran out to give her a massive hug. Before my grandpa died they used to come down to visit us all the time, but Gran's been so busy lately; travelling to all these unusual places and doing about a hundred different hobbies – computer classes and line dancing and a whole load of others.

Mum had made the most delicious tea – home-made scones with raspberry jam, and her famous marble cake – and as soon as Gran had taken off her coat and sat down at the table, we got stuck in.

"Your hair's looking very pretty, Phoebe, tied up like that," said Gran, cutting us all a huge slice of cake. "How are you getting on at drama these days? Have you sung the dreaded solo yet?"

"No, I haven't and I don't want to think about it. It was bad enough today, we had to go round the circle and say our names as loud as we could and I nearly ran out of the room when it got to my turn."

"Oh, I meant to ask you, Phoebs," said Mum. "Does Miss Howell need any help with the costumes?"

"I don't know, I'll ask her next week. But did I tell you that the hall's been painted turquoise and Miss Howell doesn't know how we're going to get it to look like a run-down, grey factory, when the whole room looks more like a scene from The Little Mermaid. You should see it, Mum. It's covered in these huge tropical fish and the turquoise is so bright it's almost blinding."

"But why does it have to look run-down if it's a dream factory?" asked Gran. "A dream factory could be brightly coloured, couldn't it?"

"No, but Baron-Von-Bolt and Ice Bomb who run the factory are greedy and they keep all the money for themselves. The factory is supposed to be in a real state and the Sweet-Dreamers are like slaves – they never have enough to eat, and their clothes are all old and tatty."

I couldn't stop talking. I think I was still excited about getting up on the stage in front of everyone without making a total idiot of myself.

"Well if the hall's turquoise, I've got a brilliant idea," said Sara, leaning forward. "She could make it an underwater factory. All the Sweet-Dreamers could be mermaids, yeah? And Baron-Von-Bolt could be a shark Gobstopper could be an octopus because he's always trying to get his hands into Baron-Von-Bolt's pockets, and I know, I know, Ice Bomb could be like a really tropical fish, because she's supposed to be beautiful. What do you think, Phoebs?"

"Oh wow, Sara! That's brilliant! You'll have to tell Miss Howell. I'm sure she'd love to hear all about *The Dream Factory* set underwater. She might even offer you a part – as a bit of seaweed."

"You're so vile!" cried Sara.

"Stop winding her up, Phoebe," said Gran, clearing the plates, but I could see she was trying not to laugh.

"Mum, is it true that Polly Carter's going to have a half-brother?" I asked, remembering what Polly said at drama. Mum's friend, Trish, lives in Polly's road and she always seem to know what's going on with everyone.

"Well, yes I think she is, but why do you want to know?"

"Oh nothing, she just mentioned it today and she seemed to be really upset."

"It's all a bit scandalous, actually," said Mum. "Apparently Polly's dad has moved in with one of the neighbours and now they're having a baby together."

"What, so you mean they're all living in the same street? That must be so awful for Polly, and her mum."

"Yes, and according to Trish there's been all sorts of carrying on. I think she said that a few weeks ago, Polly's mum threw all her dad's stuff out of the window and then tried to set fire to it on the street. The police were called and everything. God only knows what will happen when the baby's born."

"But what is a half-brother?" said Sara. "How can you have half a brother anyway? I wish I only had half a sister."

"Shut up, Sara, can't you? Your voice is actually driving me nuts. I wish I had no sister at all!"

"*Phoebe! That's horrible!*" said Mum, as

Sara stormed out of the room. "Stop picking on your sister and help me with these dishes."

While we were washing up Gran asked Mum how things were with Dad, but Mum glanced over at me and shook her head. Whatever she was going to say she obviously didn't want me to hear, but it wouldn't have made any difference. I could see how bad things were with my own eyes.

Mum was always angry or in a mood or on the verge of tears – and Dad spent more and more time at the $\mathcal{L}ife$ centre. They were barely speaking to each other at all – passing stupid messages through me and Sara, and when they did speak it nearly always ended in a row. I don't think they even knew what they were angry about any more – but it was like they'd forgotten how to communicate in any other way.

I had tried talking to Mum about Dad losing his job and about how much his work at the nursery meant to him but she wouldn't listen.

"He knows what his responsibilities are," she'd snapped. "And it's about time he lived up to them. I'm not going to support him while he goes through some kind of pathetic mid-life crisis."

The problem was I could kind of understand how both of them were feeling; I could see why Mum was cross but I knew how much Dad was missing his job at the nursery. I kept thinking there must be something I could do to get them back together, or at least get them talking again, but it was hopeless. They might not be setting fire to each other's clothes in the street, like Polly's mum – but they weren't far off.

After tea Mum said she had a headache and went upstairs to lie down for a bit while Gran got busy sorting out the ingredients for the Christmas pudding. We always make the Christmas pudding with Gran – it's like an old family tradition. We don't put money in like some people do – we add a secret ingredient, a different one every year – and Mum and Dad have to guess what it is. One year, ages and ages ago, I added chilli powder, but by mistake I put in a whole tablespoon instead of a teaspoon and Dad had to drink about a gallon of water all in one go.

"She just wanted to warm you up a bit, Robert," said Gran, as Dad's face got redder and redder, and I nearly wet myself laughing.

I was dreading Christmas this year. It was going to be totally dismal. Dad was having Christmas lunch at the Life centre – and the rest of us would probably sit around all day pretending everything was normal and fine when it so obviously wasn't. I wasn't even excited about breaking up from school. The thought of spending two weeks stuck in the house with Mum and Sara didn't exactly fill me with joy, and I wouldn't even have Star Makers to look forward to.

Gran got busy measuring out little pots of

raisins and sultanas and almonds and mixed peel and grated carrot and apple – like a Sweet-Dreamer in the factory sorting out all the ingredients for a really sweet dream. She sifted the flour and baking powder, poured in the eggs and then got me and Sara to add the little pots one at a time.

"Make sure you stir from east to west, girls," said Gran. "Or is it west to east? I can never remember. Which way did the wise men travel to see the baby Jesus?"

"How do you know they didn't walk from the North Pole to the South Pole?" said Sara, pinching raisins out of the bowl and feeding them to Barney. "Or right the way across Russia."

Gran roared with laughter. "Russia!" she spluttered. "The three wise men walking across Russia! Oh, that's priceless, Sara, absolutely priceless."

She shook her head, still chuckling to

herself. "So, what are we going to add, girls? What's our secret ingredient going to be?"

As far as I was concerned there was no point doing it – not this year when only Mum would be guessing – and no one would feel like celebrating anyway. But in the end we added molasses, a sort of sticky black treacle, and we all made a wish. I closed my eyes and concentrated really hard. I wished with every bit of strength in my body. I didn't really think it would bring Mum and Dad back together or make Polly Carter disappear in a puff of smoke *or* help me to sing my solo – but what else could I do?

An Unexpected Concert...

13

I still hadn't come up with an answer by the time I went to drama on Saturday, but I *had* decided that I was going to sing my solo. The very last part of Donny's Rise to Fame article was all about believing in yourself – and I was absolutely determined to show everyone how good I could be. I might not be able to get Mum and Dad back together or sort out Polly Carter – but surely I could sing five lines of a song without having a total nervous breakdown.

As I walked up the stairs, my determination began to drain away a little with each step. Believing in myself was a whole lot easier when I was on my own in my bedroom! Ellie was waiting for me at the top, hopping up and down.

"Quick, Phoebs, you'll never guess what!" she squealed, pulling me into the hall. "Remember last week when Arthur said he had something to tell Mandy, but he couldn't remember what it was? Well, look! It was a fair!"

She was right. The entire hall was crammed full of people; most of them very old ladies with scarves on their heads and those shopping trolleys on wheels. There were loads of stalls piled high with clothes and toys and food – and some rather droopy paper-chain decorations hanging from the ceiling – a bit like the kind we used to make ourselves at primary school.

"There's no way we'll able to rehearse today, is there," I said, secretly relieved. "Not with all this going on. Where's Miss Howell anyway?"

We looked across the hall. The turquoise wall at the back was covered in a huge poster announcing The Annual Church Christmas Fair and Miss Howell was standing in front of it, right next to a brightly coloured clownfish. Her arms were folded tightly across her chest and she looked as if she might explode, or kill someone, at any moment.

We fought our way through the crowds and shopping trolleys to ask her what was going on and as we got nearer I noticed a smaller poster stuck right underneath the big one. It said:

Star Makers
Children's Drama Club
present their
Christmas Carol Concert...
...Saturday 18th December at 11a.m.

Come and hear the voices of angels!

In each corner of the poster there was a picture of a holly leaf and right at the bottom there was a drawing of an angel with musical notes coming out of its mouth.

Ellie read the poster and looked at me, shrugging. "We haven't been practising carols. Why didn't Mandy tell us we were doing a concert?"

"I didn't tell you," Miss Howell yelled above the din, "because I didn't know. I didn't know because Arthur failed to mention that there was a Christmas fair in here today, let alone the fact that *we* were supposed to be providing the entertainment. Okay? I didn't know we were supposed to be singing, and I *truly* didn't know I could hate someone as much as I hate The Great Arthur McDermott at this precise moment in time! Any other questions?"

Her hair was jet black to match her mood and it suddenly seemed so funny, the thought of us singing carols, that I started to giggle – or maybe it was just the sheer relief that I wouldn't have to sing my solo.

"*Phoebe*, stop it," said Ellie, as Mandy stormed off muttering to herself. But then she looked at my face and a minute later we were holding onto each other in hysterics, just like we used to before Sam came along.

"Come on," Ellie gasped, tears running down her face, "I spotted some delicious-looking chocolate brownies and I've got to get one before they all go. Let's see if we can find the others and tell them what's going on."

We pushed our way back through the crowds and had just about reached the chocolate brownie stall when Sam appeared.

"Hi, Ellie, hi Phoebe, have you heard? Apparently we're angels and we're putting on a concert. Anyway, Mandy wants us all on the stage straight away and she's mad as hell."

"We know," said Ellie and they raced off together, laughing about something, while I tagged along behind, trying not to feel left out. On the stage, Monty B was telling Miss Howell about how he'd always wanted to be an angel.

"Honestly, Mandy, if I'd known about the concert, I would have brought my fairy wings. And in case you're wondering, because I know you are, the reason I've got fairy wings in the first place is because—"

"Sit down, everyone," Miss Howell said, interrupting Monty B. "For those of you who haven't read the posters stuck up all over this room and outside at the front of the building, Arthur has invited us to sing Christmas carols to the masses without actually bothering to let us know. So, any ideas? Do you all know Silent Night? Away In a Manger? *The Murder of Arthur McDermott?*"

"Well, we could sing some songs from *The Dream Factory*," said Tara. "It'll be great practice for us, Mandy. Some of us have never sung in front of an audience before and it might stop us feeling so nervous when it comes to the real thing."

Sam shook her head. "It's not very seasonal, though, is it? I mean people don't go round singing songs about nightmares and bed-bugs at Christmas."

"Oh my God, yeah, it was a nightmare for Mary!" cried Neesha. "She couldn't find anywhere to have her baby and she nearly had it on the side of the road without any of those midwife people, or magazines to read, or anything. And she probably did get bed-bugs lying down on that manky straw – I bet it was minging!"

"Well *I* was nearly born on a hill in France," said Monty B. "That's why I'm called Montgomery, because *mont* means *hill* in French."

"Why didn't they just call you Mont then?" said Neesha. "Or Hill?"

Miss Howell shook her head, smiling for the

first time. "How do we end up having these crazy conversations?" she said. "Although I actually think that might be quite a good idea to sing some songs from the show."

"But not my solo," I said, quickly. "We've never practised my solo before so there's no way I could sing it today in front of all these strangers."

Miss Howell laughed. "Don't worry, Phoebe, not your solo. But perhaps you'd like to introduce us at the beginning?"

I looked at her like she was mad. *Me? Stand up and speak in front of a room full of strangers? By myself?*

"I mean you did so well when you introduced Polly the other week, remember?"

"I'll do it with her," said Monty B leaping up. "Come on, Frankie, it'll be a laugh."

"Right then," said Miss Howell as if it was all settled. "We'll just consider this a bonus – an unexpected chance to sing in front of an audience. We'll sing *Mixing a Dream, Doing the Sweet-Dream Rap, Don't Let The Bed-Bugs Bite* and *Scream!*

Scream! is easily the best song in the show. It's about what happens when the Jelly-Skulls mess around with the Sweet-Dreamers' potions, causing children all over the world to have nightmares. One of the nightmares is about this boy who finds out he's got to be a fairy in the school play and that his costume is a frilly pink tutu.

Monty B is playing the part of the boy. He doesn't actually say anything; he just wakes up wearing the tutu, looks down at himself, and then screams in horror, while the Jelly-Skulls surround him chanting:

Michael's Joseph, Priyanka's Mary
But you my dear are the Christmas fairy.
It's not a dream, it's really true,
Here's your costume, a pink tutu!

Yes a pink tutu! Let's spread the news,
And some lovely, satin ballet shoes.
You can't wake up – it's not a dream,
You can't wake up – don't try to scream.
You can't wake up – no it's not a dream,
You can't wake up – so don't try to

SCREAM!

The chant builds up, getting louder and louder and ends with all of us letting out this huge scream. Monty B is brilliant. He makes this "horrified" face and it's so funny I have to hold my breath to stop myself from laughing every time he does it. I didn't feel like laughing now, though. I felt like running straight off the stage and out of the hall, but I was too terrified to move.

Arthur appeared about ten minutes later wearing a Father Christmas costume that was about three sizes too small and carrying a huge sack of toys over his shoulder. He rang a heavy-looking gold bell to get everyone's attention and the room fell silent.

My heart was beating so fast, I thought I was going to pass out. I looked over at Miss Howell to try and make her realize I couldn't do it, but before I could catch her eye Monty B dragged me forward.

"Ladies and Gentlemen," he said, doing this ridiculous bow. "Prepare to be dazzled – and delighted – and de...well just prepare yourselves for..." He put his hand out to me, grinning and nodding, and somehow, I really don't know how, I opened my mouth and said:

"Star Makers – Children's Drama Club!"

There was a massive cheer and Catharine walked to the front of the stage to sing Sabine's main song, *Mixing a Dream*.

She sang the first verse by herself, her voice ringing out around the hall like a *real* angel, and then the rest of us joined in with the chorus. After *Mixing a Dream* we sang *Doing the*

Sweet-Dream Rap, Don't Let the Bed-Bugs Bite, and then *Scream!*

By the end of the song everyone in the hall was hysterical and Monty B got the loudest cheer. He started bowing and blowing kisses at all the old ladies and getting totally carried away until Miss Howell rushed on the stage and grabbed him.

"Thank you. Thank you so much," she said, turning to give us all a clap. "Now don't forget to come and see *The Dream Factory*, our fantastic show, on the 21st of February. And a very happy Christmas to everyone."

Monty B started blowing kisses again and Miss Howell pulled him off the stage, laughing. "Monty B! You're a liability," she gasped. "I swear I'll be grey by the time we've finished this production!"

"What does liability mean? Is it a compliment?"

Catharine threw her arms round him. "It

means you're bad news," she cried, "but we all love you anyway!"

"Fantastic, Phoebe!" said Miss Howell, coming over to give me a hug. "I knew you could do it."

"Oh, thank you, *Mandy*," I said, without thinking, and then rushed to the back of the stage before she could see that my face was roughly the same colour as Monty B's hair.

It was probably stupid to get so excited about speaking in front of a bunch of strangers and singing a few songs from the show, but when everyone cheered at the end my arms went all goose-pimply and I couldn't stop grinning.

"How cool was that, Frankie?" said Monty B.

"Really cool," I said, and smiled at him. A proper smile; not twisted up or anything.

I looked around at everyone on the stage; at Ellie and Sam and Neesha and Catharine and Tara. A few months ago, when I first joined

Star Makers, I didn't know what I was doing there, or how I was ever going to fit in. These days I couldn't imagine anywhere else in the world that I'd rather be.

Time to Get Serious!

The holiday seemed to drag on for ever and it was such a relief when it was finally over. Christmas was just as awful as I thought it was going to be; Mum was in the worst mood ever and Dad spent all his time at the *Life* centre. I was so desperate to get out of the house that I didn't even feel too bad about going back to school. I wasn't exactly looking forward to it – but it had to be better than staying at home.

I was *really* excited about going back to drama but I still didn't know what I was going to do about my solo. Donny made it sound so simple in the self-belief section of his article. All you had to do was repeat this special mantra about 150 times a day and success would be

yours. It went something like: *I am truly gifted.*
I can be anything that I want to be. Nothing
can stand in my way.

I had planned to say it every morning before
I went down for breakfast but then the first day
I actually tried it Sara walked past my room
and nearly wet herself laughing.

"You *are* truly gifted," she shouted out,
banging on the door. "Truly gifted at being
truly stupid!" And then I remembered, way too
late, that I wasn't going to follow Donny's
advice any more.

"I hope you all had a fantastic break,"
Mandy greeted us on our first Saturday back,
"but after today I don't want to see anyone
using a script."

"Oh my God, Mandy! You're having a laugh,"
groaned Neesha.

"No, Neesha, I'm not *having a laugh*, as you
put it. It's not funny! There are only four more
Saturdays until the dress rehearsal, and the

best way to feel really secure about your part is to stop relying on your script.

"Anyway," she added, with a twinkly smile, "I'm sure you all spent heaps of time during the holidays going over your lines so it shouldn't be too much of a problem."

"I just don't know what happened to *my* script, Mandy," Ellie cried suddenly, ripping open her bag and chucking everything up in the air. "I lost it right at the beginning of the holidays so I haven't been able to learn my lines at all."

"Now why doesn't that surprise me?" said Mandy. "Have you checked the hamster cage?"

"I know all my lines, in Act One *and* Act Two," said Sam, smugly.

I knew all of mine as well, but I didn't say anything. It wasn't going to be much use if I was too scared to sing my solo at the end.

"Right, let's make a start," said Mandy.

"Everyone turn to Act Two, Scene One and I want all of you on the stage."

We ran through the scene a few times, ending with the Sweet-Dreamers singing, *Don't Let the Bed-Bugs Bite*, the song we'd practised over at Ellie's house weeks and weeks ago.

"Sing up," Mandy called out. "I can't believe that's the loudest sound you can make. Come on Ellie, open your mouth! All of you – sing from your bellies. Tara! What *are* you doing? You keep turning the opposite way to everyone else!"

"It's no use, Mandy," Tara wailed. "I can't do it. The message from my brain doesn't reach my feet. I know I should be turning one way, but my feet keep turning me round the other way." She glared down at her disobedient feet through her small, round glasses.

"Phoebe, why don't you stand next to Tara and help her? You seem to know all the dances really well."

My face started to burn up. Me help Tara? How was I supposed to help Tara – brains of the class – Perkins?

"Come on, quickly, Phoebe. Show her which way to turn."

I shuffled over to Tara and stood to her right.

"Erm, it's quite easy really," I said, as if I knew what I was talking about. "All you have to do is to make sure that every time you turn, you turn towards me. And make sure your left shoulder turns towards the audience first."

"Gosh, thanks, Phoebe," she said after we'd tried it out a few times. "I wish I was as good at dancing as you are, but I'm completely useless. Did you have dance lessons before you joined Star Makers?"

"No, of course not. I never did *anything* before I joined Star Makers. I don't mean I didn't do *anything*...of course I did things like go to school and brush my teeth and stuff...just

not singing or dancing or anything like that..."
I trailed off blushing again.

Tara started to giggle, but I thought she looked a bit alarmed. *Go to school and brush my teeth?* I was the one who needed help!

At break time Mandy called us over one at a time to measure us for costumes. She'd made the Sweet-Dreamer girls these dingy-looking old dresses with patches on but she needed to sort out the different lengths.

"How was your holiday, Phoebe?" she asked, as she measured me from the back of my shoulder down to my knee. Then she turned me round and looked at me more closely. "Are you okay, sweetheart? You look exhausted. Look at those bags under your eyes. Is everything all right?"

"Yes, everything's fine," I lied.

"What about Christmas Day? Did you do anything special?"

"No, nothing that special really."

What would I say anyway? That my dad who's now called Eagle Dust, had lunch with a load of people I've never even met – and that my mum stayed in her dressing gown for most of the day, moping around like she was at a funeral. It was so much easier to keep quiet.

I went back over to the others, but when it was time to start again I couldn't find my script anywhere. I knew I'd left it in my bag, I could remember putting it in there when Mandy called me over – but it definitely wasn't there now. I asked Ellie and Sam if they'd seen it and Ellie helped me hunt around a bit – but it had completely disappeared.

I was just about to ask Mandy what I should do when Monty B came bounding over. "I'll help you find it, Frankie," he cried, pulling me across the hall.

And then Polly called out in like The Loudest Voice Ever, "*Oh Frankie, off to practise your kissing scenes?*"

I yanked my arm away from Monty B and ran out to the toilets. I could hear Polly making kissing noises behind me as I fled – and my face was on fire. I stayed in the loo for ages thinking about how much I hated Polly Carter and about how obvious it was that she'd taken my script and hidden it somewhere, but there was no way I could prove it. I walked round and round the tiny toilet cubicle trying to work out what I should do. I really didn't want to go back inside – but there didn't seem to be any alternative.

"Look, I've found your script, Phoebs," said Ellie the second I walked through the doors. "It was stuffed right down behind the radiator."

I looked across the hall at Polly sniggering with her friends. I knew I should tell Mandy, but the thought of her making a big thing out of it in front of everyone, asking if anyone knew anything, was even worse. And anyway, it's not as if Polly was going to come clean. I mean there was more chance of me singing my solo than of her owning up and saying she did it. I managed to stay out of her way for the rest of the session but I knew I'd have to face up to the situation sooner or later.

On Thursday Dad came to meet me from school. Ever since that day when he talked to me about losing his job – he's been turning up once or twice a week to walk me home. He never comes in – so Mum doesn't know – but it's not like it's a really big secret or anything.

We walked along in silence for a few minutes and then he started to tell me about this couple he'd met over Christmas at the $\mathcal{Life}$ centre, and the problems they'd been having in their marriage. I didn't really get why he was bothering to tell me about two people I'd never even met, but after a bit I wondered if he might be trying to tell me something without actually telling me; like some hidden clue about him and Mum. He'd just got to a really good bit about how the centre was helping them to work things out when we saw beaky-nose Burton coming towards us and we both groaned.

"It's absolutely disgusting," she shouted, striding towards us. "There's still rubbish in the bins and it's been *how* many days since Christmas? I don't know why we bother paying our council tax, I really don't. And have you noticed that some people are *not* using their recycling boxes?"

"I'm so sorry, Valerie," said Dad waving his arm at her, "but we really can't stop. We're right in the middle of a deep, transcendental meditation and any sudden or unexpected disturbances might be fatal."

Valerie opened her mouth and then shut it again and then opened it again but nothing came out. As we walked past her, Dad started to hum and I joined in trying to keep a straight face. I didn't even know what transcendental meditation was but it was the first time I'd ever seen Valerie Burton lost for words and I felt like cheering or something. Dad looked over at me and smiled mid-hum, and just for a second it was like it used to be before everything went wrong.

The following Saturday Mandy arrived with some of the costumes.

"Pop into the toilets with these," she said, handing them round. "I've made three basic sizes so I might need to adjust some of them. The boys have got trousers to match the dresses and this is your Gobstopper costume, Polly." She handed Polly a black, silky jumpsuit. "The rest of the costumes will be ready next week."

"There is no way I'm wearing this!" cried Polly, screwing up her face and holding the jumpsuit out in front of her as if it was diseased or something.

"What do you mean?" said Mandy. "It's a fantastic costume!"

"But I'll look so stupid!"

"No more stupid than usual," said Monty B to Adam.

Polly opened her mouth to say something back but Mandy put her hands on her shoulders and steered her towards the door. "Come on, madam. Into the toilets and then pop out and show me when you've got it on."

We all squashed into the loos to try on the dresses. Polly moaned and groaned about her jumpsuit but then decided it looked quite cool and paraded around the hall showing it off to everyone. There were a few alterations to make but when Mandy had finished pinning hems and adjusting some of the waistbands she hung them on the clothes rail at the back of the stage. Then we ran right through Act One with no scripts, and considering how bad we were before Christmas it was nothing short of a miracle.

"That was great, guys," Mandy said when

we got to the end. "It's really beginning to take shape. Next week we'll run through Act Two with no scripts and start to think about bows and an encore."

"Oh I love the bows," trilled Sam. "It's the best bit. Everyone cheers and once, at the end of this play I was in, I even got a standing ovation."

I didn't even know what a standing ovation was but it was obviously something *amazing*.

"Are you sure they weren't just standing up to leave?" said Monty B, and he winked at Mandy.

"Well done those of you who didn't need prompting today," said Mandy, trying not to laugh. "But those of you who did – get working!"

Just then Arthur turned up, and we finally found out why he'd had the hall painted turquoise. His amateur dramatics group, The

Players, were putting on a play in two weeks' time and it was called *The Ocean Deep*.

"Actually, Mandy, my dear," he said. "The play has nothing to do with the depth of the ocean at all – it's about the deep, dark recesses of the human mind. The word ocean therefore, in this sense, is simply a metaphor."

"Fabulous," said Mandy, a fixed smile on her face. "But you do know, Arthur, that we're only weeks away from *our* show and you wouldn't believe how hard all the children are working. So just as long as it doesn't interfere with any of my rehearsals, *or* the deep, dark recesses of *my* mind, eh?"

"Interfere!" Arthur roared, looking particularly deranged. "Of course it won't interfere." And with a quick tug of his beard, he strode out of the room.

Monty B had stayed right out of my way since Polly and the kissing comment. I still caught him staring at me when he thought I wasn't looking – but he hadn't actually spoken to me or anything. I half-wanted to tell him what was going on with Polly. I just had this mad idea that if I told him *everything* we'd be able to work out a plan to get rid of her together. But then something terrible happened – and sorting out Polly Carter didn't seem to matter at all.

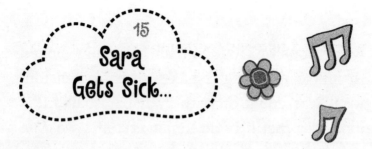

15
Sara
Gets Sick...

Sara started to feel ill at teatime the following Thursday. She threw up a couple of times and went to bed early. Her temperature shot up during the night and at about three o'clock Mum called an ambulance. She then rang Dad to come and stay with me, and by the time the ambulance arrived Sara was whimpering and her back and legs were covered in a horrible, purply red rash.

Dad and I sat in the kitchen drinking tea and staring at the walls, and after what seemed like an age Mum rang Dad from the hospital and told him that it was suspected meningitis. I didn't even know what meningitis was exactly, but I knew you could die from it and when Dad told me I burst out crying. I couldn't remember the last time I'd said anything even a little bit nice to Sara and now she was in hospital dying!

Dad called Gran and as soon as she arrived we all went up to see Sara.

"It's only *suspected* meningitis," Dad kept saying in the car. "We've got to hang on to that thought and stay positive. That's what Sara needs from us right now, Phoebs, lots of positive thoughts."

But it was a total nightmare. We sat around for hours and hours and hardly anyone would tell us what was going on or even talk to us. Mum was allowed in the room with Sara but every time she came out she was crying so much I couldn't understand anything she said. Her eyes were so swollen up and puffy they were almost closed. The only words I could hear were, "My precious baby, my precious baby," and every time she said it I started to cry again.

I was sort of starving as well, but there was nothing to eat and I was pretty sure I wouldn't be able to swallow anything anyway. My throat felt completely stuffed up, like how the toilet gets sometimes when Sara uses too much loo paper. I sat there on this hard, plastic chair and thought about how I was going to make it up to her when she got better. I'd let her do anything she wanted: borrow my clothes, use my make-up, I'd even let her come in my room and listen to my Donny Dallesio CDs. I'd be the best big sister in the world.

We sat and sat; hour after hour. The time crawled by so slowly I wanted to scream. At one point I thought I must be going mad or hallucinating or something because I caught a glimpse of Polly Carter at the end of the corridor clutching hold of a helium balloon. I shrank back in my chair so that she wouldn't notice me – she was the last person I wanted to see. Her dad was walking behind her hurrying her along and she looked as miserable as ever.

I blinked really hard and when I looked again she was gone. I wondered if I'd imagined the whole thing – I mean what were the chances of her being here on the same day as me anyway? But then I remembered about her half-brother. People always bought those helium balloons to the hospital when a new baby was born. I bet that's why she looked so miserable; she was probably worried that her dad might love the new baby more than he loved her. I couldn't even imagine how I'd feel if my dad went off and had a baby with someone new.

"I'll just go and find us some sandwiches or something," Gran said, after another hour had crawled by. "What do you want, Phoebe? Cheese? Tuna?"

I shook my head. "I am hungry, Gran, but my throat's all stuffed up. I don't think I could even manage a packet of crisps."

Dad popped his head round the door to ask

Mum if she wanted a sandwich but she just hissed something at him. I couldn't hear what it was – but it sounded bad.

"Just a simple, 'no thank you' would do," Dad muttered turning away from the door; and then Mum came storming out.

"What the hell's the matter with you?" she spat. "Is this really the time to be worried about sandwiches and manners and rubbish like that? Just do me a favour and leave me alone can't you! Why do you have to be so utterly useless? I'm sick of the sight of you!"

My tummy twisted up into the tightest knot and I felt like bashing their heads together. That's what Mum always says to me and Sara when we argue over something. You'd think in a situation as awful as this they'd be able to get on for Sara's sake – even if it was only for a few, measly hours.

When Gran went off to get the sandwiches I told Dad I needed the loo and I slipped off to see if I could find Polly. I don't even know why but it was like seeing her here at the hospital was completely different from seeing her at school or at drama. It was like being trapped in some sort of twilight zone where absolutely anything could happen.

It took ages and ages but eventually I found her sitting at the end of a long corridor. She was holding her balloon in one hand and her phone in the other, staring at the screen as if it might have the answer to something.

"Hey, Polly," I said, walking up to her. "Has your new brother been born?"

"*Half*-brother," she snapped, not really looking at me. "What are you doing here anyway?"

"My sister's sick. She might be dying." I don't know why I told her. I don't even know why I'd bothered to find her in the first place – it's not as if she was going to care. It's just that I was so tired and feeling so bad about everything. I *nearly* said, "Don't worry about your dad loving the new baby more than you," but I knew it would sound pathetic so I just stood there.

"Sorry about your sister," Polly said after a bit. She looked at me for a second and then back at her phone. "I hope she gets better."

I sat down next to her. "What are you doing anyway?"

"Nothing really, just playing some dumb game to pass the time. I didn't even want to come, but my dad forced me."

"Do your mum and dad get on any more?" I said. "My mum and dad are barely talking to each other."

She stabbed at the phone, keeping her eyes fixed firmly on the game. "My mum *hates* my dad and my dad is so busy with his new girlfriend he doesn't even notice I'm there half the time. He'd much rather have a brand-new baby than be stuck with me."

Suddenly I felt really sorry for her. It was crazy but I couldn't help it. We sat there for a bit longer taking turns on her phone. I didn't have a clue what the game was about – I was way too tired and worried to concentrate, but it was better than doing nothing.

After a bit Polly's dad came over and took her in to see the new baby.

"See you, then," she said, trailing after him with her balloon. Then just before she got to the door she turned round and said, "Sorry about your script, Phoebe. I only did it to make the others laugh." And she disappeared behind the blue, hospital doors.

I sat there in a daze. I couldn't believe it. I thought about how every time Polly said something nasty to me, she was nearly always surrounded by her mates – and they were always laughing and sniggering as if she was the cleverest person alive. All this time I was convinced she hated me – but maybe she thought that being mean to me was the only way to impress her friends and keep them hanging round.

I went back to find Gran and Dad, going over and over what Polly had said. I knew I should hate her but I couldn't. It's not like we were going to be best friends or anything but at least I kind of knew why she'd been so vile to me.

Finally at about six in the evening a doctor came out to talk to us about Sara.

"You've got a real fighter on your hands there," he said, sort of smiling but not really, "and I'm delighted to say that we've had the test results back and it's viral meningitis not bacterial."

"What does that mean exactly?" said Gran, her voice shaking a bit.

"Well, we've done a lumber punch, that was the big injection in her spine, and the fluid has come back clear. She's got a nasty virus and she's not out of the woods yet, but thankfully it's not as serious as we first thought. She's got to have lots of rest but like I said, she's a fighter and there's no reason why she shouldn't make a full recovery."

I felt so proud when he said that, about her being a fighter. I wanted to cheer or something, but I was too tired.

"Now I know it's difficult but I think it would be best if you were to go home and get a good night's sleep and then come back in the morning."

Dad ended up staying at the hospital with Mum and I went home with Gran.

When we got in I ran straight up to Sara's room to get Barney. Gran started to make me some cheese on toast but I fell asleep on the couch – cuddled up with Barney – and slept there right through to the morning.

I woke up when the phone rang. It was Mum. She said Sara had improved lots over night but that we wouldn't be able to visit until later – then she started to cry again and I couldn't understand the rest. I texted Ellie to let her know I wouldn't be coming to drama, and then after breakfast we went up to the High Road to get some tastier food to take to the hospital.

"Is everything okay?" Mrs. Burton called out as we passed her house. "Only I saw the ambulance arrive in the early hours and I've been worried sick. I don't think my eyes closed for more than five minutes all night long."

"Thanks for your concern," said Gran, speeding up, "but everything's fine."

Suddenly I thought about Dad humming the other day and I started to giggle.

"What's so funny, Phoebs?" said Gran.

"It was Dad," I said. "Mrs. Burton was going on and on about the rubbish and the Council and stuff and he pretended we were in the middle of a deep transcendental meditation or something and then we both walked past her humming. Honestly, Gran, it was so funny, you should've seen her face."

Gran linked arms with me, chuckling, and for a tiny moment I pretended it was a normal day and we were just popping up to the shops to get something for lunch.

"We must remember to take Barney up to the hospital," I said, cuddling in to Gran. "If Sara wakes up she won't understand where he is. You know she's never spent a night away from him before and she'll be so frightened."

"Don't worry, love. We'll take him up a bit later. Everything's going to be all right. You'll see."

16
Missing Costumes!

Sara stayed in hospital for a few more days before they let her come home. Mum and Dad spent loads of time up there together but it didn't seem to help them get on. By the time Mum brought Sara home they were more or less ignoring each other and I couldn't imagine how they were ever going to sort things out.

Mum seemed to blame Dad for everything. She went on and on and on about how selfish he was and how he should grow up and get a proper job so that she didn't have to worry about everything all the time. But Dad didn't say anything to defend himself or explain *why* it was so difficult for him to find a new job, he just spent more and more time at the *Life* centre and less and less time with us.

When I got to Star Makers on Saturday, Mandy was busy handing out the rest of the costumes and it was such a relief to be back with everyone and away from all the dramas at home.

Adam had already changed into his costume and he looked amazing. He was wearing a really smart silver suit, a dark blue tie covered in silver stars and big silver boots. Neesha and the other Jelly-Skulls had black tops with a white outline of a skull on the front, and Monty B was prancing about in his pink tutu. But Sam looked the best. She had a blonde wig, these long, silver, high-heeled boots and a tiny, silver mini-dress.

"Hey! Don't even think about messing with the Ice Bomb," she snarled, teetering around in her heels like a top fashion model.

"Oh, you all look fantastic," Mandy said, excitedly. "Adam and Monty B, pop onto the stage, will you, and get the other costumes down. I'd like to see you all in your costumes just once so that I know everything's sorted for next week."

Adam and Monty B jumped onto the stage and disappeared behind the velvet curtains, a cloud of dust rising up behind them.

"I'm just going to the loo to do my wig," said Sam, and she staggered out of the room on her high-heels holding on to Ellie for support.

"Hey, Mandy, we can't see any dresses up here," Adam called out a few seconds later.

Mandy ran her hand through her hair, which was a sort of dark purple colour and very spiky. "They're on the rail, boys, remember? Right at the back."

"No, the *rail's* here," Monty B popped his head back through the curtain, "but there are no dresses on it."

"Of course they're there," Mandy muttered. "Where else would they be?"

She jumped onto the stage and then leaped straight off again, out through the double-doors and down the corridor to Arthur's office. A minute later she stormed back into the hall with Arthur following a few steps behind. He had a hot drink in his hand and his beard was full of flaked-off bits of sausage roll or something.

"*BUT ARTHUR! WHAT DO YOU MEAN THEY MUST HAVE BEEN SOLD?*" she shouted, waving her arms about, and for a second I was sure she was going to hit him. "*WHO IN THEIR RIGHT MINDS WOULD WANT TO BUY A BUNCH OF OLD PATCHED-UP DRESSES?*"

"I really *am* sorry, Mandy," said Arthur, trying to walk out of the room backwards. "But you see, you err…left them on the stage and so Mrs. Beagle from the church fund-raising committee…erm…just assumed, erroneously as it turns out, that they'd been put there as part of the church jumble sale we had last Sunday. You surely must have noticed that there were lots of other old clothes up there stuffed into bags?" He took a few more steps back, muttering something about *all being fair in love and show business*.

"I just can't believe I'm hearing this," said Mandy. "Do you realize how much work went into making those dresses? There's no way I can make them again before the production. The dress rehearsal is *next week* for goodness' sake." She looked close to tears.

"What's going on?" Sam asked me, as she came back from the toilet.

"I'm not really sure, but it sounds as if someone called Mrs. Beagle sold all our costumes at the church jumble sale last Sunday afternoon."

"No way! Who would want to buy some tatty, old dresses and trousers with patches sewn on?"

Mandy was still shouting at Arthur when he said he could hear the phone ringing in his office and practically skipped out of the room shouting, "The bells! The bells!"

"I must have done something really awful in another life to deserve this." Mandy sighed, and then suddenly, without any warning at all, she threw back her head and started to laugh – but not in a funny ha ha sort of way; more in the way of someone who's finally lost their mind. She bent over, clutching hold of her stomach and groaning, and I wondered if one of us should call an ambulance.

"There must be another hall we could use," she gasped, wiping her eyes. "There must, because I'm going to end up murdering that man if we stay here, I really am. Come on, everyone, let's sit down and try to work out what we're going to do."

"Well, my mum's really good at sewing, Mandy," I blurted out without even thinking. My face turned scarlet and everyone looked at me.

"Is she, Phoebe?" said Mandy. She'd stopped laughing now except for the odd snort.

"Yes, she's really good. She makes wedding dresses and stuff, but I'm not sure if she's actually free today because my sister isn't very well…and…" I trailed off, fiddling with my script. It still felt weird calling Miss Howell, Mandy, and that was the most I'd ever said in front of everyone at drama. I looked down at my hands, willing my face to return to its normal colour.

"Well, is there anyone else?" Mandy looked around the circle. "We need ten dresses and three pairs of trousers, so that's going to be way too much for one person."

"There's always my nan," Monty B said. "She's brilliant at knitting but she's very slow. She started knitting me this scarf about three years ago and she still hasn't finished. She says it might be ready by the time I get married! She's even going to sew on little reflector lights to keep me safe in the winter."

"Ah, bless," said Neesha.

"Oh, that reminds me, actually," said Ellie. "My dad's a stage technician thingy and he said he'd be happy to come and help out with the lights if you want him to."

"Do we ever! That would be fantastic, Ellie. I was going to attempt the lights myself, but then Arthur mentioned that he was a bit of a whiz at special effects and you can just imagine how thrilled I was about that! I'll give your dad a ring later.

"Okay, let's move on. We need to have a full run-through today. It's our last chance before the dress rehearsal. I don't want to see any scripts at all and I want a massive effort from everyone. No talking in between scenes, and try to be ready for your next entrance without me having to tell you.

"I'll try to get hold of your mum a bit later, Phoebe, to see if she can come to the rescue. And maybe Monty's nan will be able to help out too."

The run-through went quite well even though Mandy did keep stopping us, reminding us to speak up, to sing from our bellies, to space ourselves properly and to make eye contact with the audience. We only managed Act One before the break and I said a little prayer that we wouldn't get to the end of Act Two, which was stupid really, because I was going to have to face up to my solo situation at some point. I had planned to talk to Mandy about it today, but there was no way I could mention it now that half the costumes had gone missing.

I was also going to ask Polly about her new brother, but as soon as I saw her at school on Monday, back with her friends whispering about something, their heads close together, I knew there was no way I was going to say anything. She hadn't actually been horrible to me since the hospital, but then she hadn't been particularly nice either. I looked across at her now. She was on the other side of the hall mucking about – acting like she didn't have a care in the world – but I knew she was covering up how she really felt.

In the break Mandy called Mum. I was sure she'd say she couldn't help out because she had Sara at home in bed recovering from a serious illness, and because the rest of the family was in pieces. But she didn't. According to Mandy, she said she'd love to help, but everyone would have to come over to ours because she couldn't leave Sara: *anything* to pretend things were normal!

As it turned out we didn't get to my solo in the end but we were getting closer and closer and I knew I couldn't avoid it for ever.

"There's just one more thing," Mandy said before we went home. "The tickets are on sale from me. We're doing three performances so you really must try to get as many people as you can to come along. Adam's designed this brilliant poster for us to put up at school, and in the library, and other places like that – and I'll give some leaflets out to each of you next week. There's nothing worse than performing to a half-empty hall."

Except performing to a FULL one, I thought, but I didn't say anything.

"Why did you invite everyone round to ours when Sara's so ill and everything?" I asked Mum the second Dad dropped me home.

She looked at me, bewildered, as if I was speaking in a different language or something. "I did it for you, Phoebs, to help out. Miss Howell said *you'd* suggested it, and after everything that's happened, with Sara and the hospital, I just wanted to...you know...do something for *you*. I even borrowed an extra machine from Mrs. Burton!"

I stood there thinking of all the things she could have done for me, like sort things out with Dad for a start. Their rows were getting worse and worse and I was dead scared that the further they grew apart, the harder it was going to be for them to get back together. So it's not as if offering to sew a few costumes was going to magically put things right.

17

Rats Don't Burp!

I trudged upstairs and shut myself in my room. I couldn't believe that Monty B *and* Mandy were coming over – it was so embarrassing. I wouldn't be able to think of anything to say, and if Mum let Sara come down she'd probably go on and on about Monty B being my boyfriend or something.

I flopped down on my bed and stared at my poster of Donny. Sometimes I imagined him walking straight out of the poster and into my room. It would be so amazing if he could. I'd be able to ask him loads of stuff – like how I was ever going to find the courage to sing my solo for a start. Except knowing him he'd probably tell me to stick a smile on my face, slap a load of gel on my head and then repeat some ridiculous mantra.

"I am the World's Greatest Singer!" I said to myself, just for a joke. "I am the World's Greatest Singer and no one else in the Whole Entire Universe *or* Star Makers Drama Club can sing anywhere near as well as—"

"Get that, will you, Phoebe?" Mum called out, interrupting me mid-mantra. "I'm just taking Sara's temperature and someone's at the door."

I ran a brush through my hair and traipsed back downstairs. Mum had cleared a huge space in the living room and set up *her* sewing machine on one side – and the one she'd borrowed from Mrs. Burton on the other.

"Hi, Frankie," said Monty B, coming in with his nan. "This is going to be so cool."

Just then Mum came down from Sara's room. "Why don't you and Monty B go and sort out some tea while we wait for Mandy to arrive," she said, taking Monty B's nan into the living room.

In the kitchen I turned on the kettle and reached up to get some mugs down.

"How's your sister, by the way?" said Monty B, helping himself to a biscuit. "Ellie said she was really ill."

"She was but she's much better now. Hey, you'll never guess who I saw when I was up at the hospital? Polly Carter. Her new brother had just been born and she was visiting him."

Monty B pulled a face and stuffed another biscuit in his mouth. "Imagine having her as a sister. I think I'd rather be an only child!"

"Don't say that. She's not that bad!"

"*What?* Did someone drop a brick on your head or something, Phoebe Franks? This is Polly Carter we're talking about. Has your mum taken *your* temperature lately?" He came over and put his hand on my head. "Cool as a cucumber! So if you're not ill you're obviously bonkers." Suddenly he lurched towards the door and grabbed the handle as if he was trying to escape. "Help me! Please, somebody, help me! I'm trapped in the room with a madwoman – let me out!"

He stopped when he saw my face. "Sorry, Frankie. This is serious. I get it, really."

"It's *really* serious. She's been on my case ever since I started at Woodville but I've never told *anyone,* and then at the hospital she sort of said sorry, well not really, but she said she just did stuff to me to make her friends laugh. But there's more to it than that, I know there is. Anyway, I don't want you to tell anyone because since then she hasn't actually done anything and I think deep down she feels really bad."

I looked over at Monty B. I knew he was an idiot, but it was such a relief to tell someone about Polly after all this time.

"You really are bonkers if you think she's

sorry, Frankie, but I won't say anything, I swear. Next time she does something, though – you tell me and I'll sort her out for you. You can always rely on me," he said, doing a silly salute. And in a funny sort of way I knew I could.

We went back inside with the tea and a plate of biscuits and got to work on the costumes. Mandy had arrived and she was laying everything out on the floor. Monty B and I were going to pin the patterns onto the material, Monty B's nan was going to cut them out, and Mandy and Mum were going to do all the sewing. We worked non-stop for two hours and then took a break to have something to eat. Mum carried Sara down from her room and laid her on the couch and then ordered a Chinese takeaway from up the road.

Everyone made a huge fuss over Sara and she just loved being the centre of attention. She couldn't stop talking to Monty B either, just went on and on telling him about the hospital and the huge injection she had in her back and about how she couldn't wait to start drama and I could tell Monty B thought she was fantastic. Everyone always does.

Then all of a sudden, with no warning at all, Sara grabbed Monty B's arm and said, "But I've got to tell you the funniest thing, Monty B. Do you remember that day when Phoebe gelled back her hair, and there were bits of tissue stuck in it, you know that day when you came round to give her a lift to drama. Well—"

"Hey, I bet you didn't know," I interrupted in a really loud voice. I had no idea what I was going to say next, but I knew I had to shut Sara up. "I bet you didn't know that...that..." I searched my brain for something to say. *Anything*. Everyone stopped eating and looked at me. There *had* to be something there, some nonsense hidden away in my head that I could waffle on about.

And then suddenly I remembered this one

time Donny got to meet the Queen at this special awards ceremony. In this interview he gave he said he was so nervous that he ended up saying, "Your Majesty, it's an honour to meet you. And did you know, Ma'am, that the average person uses approximately fifty-seven sheets of toilet paper a day."

I knew exactly how he felt. This was even worse than meeting the Queen. Everyone was waiting, and I knew that if I didn't speak Sara was going to say something totally humiliating about me and Monty B.

"Er...I bet you didn't know," I said, "that it's actually impossible to stick your elbow into your ear, hahaha, or that, er...when an armadillo digs a hole it can hold its breath for up to six whole minutes without dying."

For a moment no one said anything at all, they just looked at me as if I'd finally cracked, but then Monty B started to laugh.

"Oh that's brilliant, Frankie," he spluttered,

bits of sweet and sour chicken balls flying across the table. "That's so random; I swear I'm going to choke in a minute."

"And I bet you didn't know," I said, unable to stop now I'd started, "that a giraffe is the only animal that can clean its ears with its own tongue. Or that rats can't burp."

I thought Monty B was going to fall off his chair – he was gasping and groaning and clutching his stomach and it was so funny I started to laugh with him.

"They're like a double act, these two are," said Monty B's nan, and for some reason that made me laugh even more.

I don't even know where all that stuff came from; it must have been buried deep in my brain somewhere just waiting to come out. I laughed so much I thought I was going to throw up or wet myself or something and then when I stopped laughing I realized I was starving. I ate about three spring rolls in a row and for the first time since Sara was rushed to hospital my throat didn't feel clogged up at all.

After tea, Mum opened a bottle of red wine for the grown-ups and we carried on cutting, pinning and sewing until about nine. The later it got, the more giggly everyone became, and at one point Mandy leaped up and did this hilarious impression of Arthur swinging his cape and pulling at his beard which had us all in stitches.

"You know what, Mandy?" Mum said, laughing so much she was almost hysterical. Her words were slurred and I think she was a bit drunk. "I really do admire you; working all week as a teacher, and then spending your weekends with kids as well. Whatever possessed you to start up the group in the first place?" She took another big swig of wine. "You are either a living saint or completely insane."

"Oh no, there was nothing saintly about it, Maxine," said Mandy. "More to do with the end of a bad relationship. After spending months waiting for my phone to ring, I decided it was time to get off my backside and do something for myself. So it's the demon Declan you should be thanking, not me."

She grabbed one of the Sweet-Dreamer dresses. "And here I am, six months later, spending my Saturday night remaking a bunch of costumes after the first lot were sold by Mrs. Beagle at a church fund-raising sale, and wondering how I could get away with murder!"

"And who says the glamour's gone out of show business?" said Monty B's nan, and we all burst out laughing again.

Finally, all thirteen costumes were finished. Mandy got up and stretched. "I can't believe we've done it. I'll have to sew on some patches but I can sort that out during the week. Thank you all so, so much. I can't tell you how much I appreciate your help and I'm not going to let these costumes out of my sight for a second!"

When everyone had gone home Mum poured herself another glass of wine and sat down on the edge of the couch. Sara was upstairs asleep and the house was suddenly very quiet after all the laughing and mucking about.

"I'll just clear up shall I?" I said, but Mum didn't answer. I began to pick up the scraps of material and thread that were scattered all over the floor. I crawled around the room while Mum just sat there staring into her wine and neither of us said a word. She was so still it was creepy.

"You know I don't think Mandy could've done it without you, Mum," I said after a bit. "And it was nice to see Monty B's nan again, wasn't it?"

But she didn't say anything. She just sat there staring into her glass. I put all the scraps into a plastic bag and I was just by the door about to go upstairs when she made this sort of horrible gasping noise, like she couldn't breathe properly. I swung back round and she was looking right at me.

"I think I've lost Dad for ever, Phoebs," she sobbed.

"No, don't say that, Mum." I dropped the bag and rushed across to her.

"I have. I've lost him for ever. And do you want to know the funniest thing? He's the only man I've ever loved. I was sixteen when we met, you know; still at school. That means I've loved him for more than half my life. And there's never been anyone else, not in all that time. But have you seen the way he looks at me, Phoebe? Like I'm not even there. Like I'm just some person he used to know."

She was waving her glass about and the wine was sloshing all over her lap. I kneeled down in front of her and took the glass out of her hand. "You haven't lost him – what are you talking about? He still loves you, Mum, I know he does. Look, why don't you phone him? Or I

223

could phone him if you want? I'll try to arrange a meeting – a proper one. You just need to talk to each other."

"I couldn't cope with him moping around all the time. There was no money and he wouldn't sort himself out and it went on and on while I was trying to keep everything together. It was me who had to take on extra shifts at the Co-op whilst he just kept moaning about losing his precious job." She slumped back into the sofa, shaking her head from side to side. "I never wanted to hurt anyone, but it was like having three children instead of two. You do understand, don't you, Phoebe?"

She held her hands out to me and I climbed onto her lap, curling myself into a ball. I couldn't even remember the last time we'd had a cuddle, not a proper one.

"You're such a good girl, Phoebs," she whispered into my hair. "I love you so much."

Later on in bed, wide awake, clutching my

special shell, I realized that there was only one person who could get Mum and Dad talking again.

"They don't call me Phoebe Franks Super-Sorter for nothing," I whispered into the darkness. Of course they don't call me Phoebe Franks Super-Sorter at all, whoever *they* are, but I wasn't about to let a little thing like that stop me!

18
A Star in the Making...

When we arrived at drama for the dress rehearsal the following Saturday, the hall was full of people getting ready for an evening performance of *The Ocean Deep* or whatever Arthur's play was called.

Arthur himself was nowhere in sight and Mandy was trying to explain to one of the guys there, as patiently as she could, that this was our one and only opportunity for a dress rehearsal. We started to get changed anyway. Tara Perkins's mum and Catharine's older sister had arrived early to help with hair and make-up.

The Sweet-Dreamers had to wear foundation, eyeliner and some red face paint to make their cheeks rosy. But the Jelly-Skulls had to look really scary, so they were having the outline of a skull drawn on their faces, and their hair back-combed with loads of hairspray to make it stand on end.

I hardly recognized myself in the mirror when Tara's mum had finished with me. My freckles were all covered up for a start and I wondered if there was some magic cream or operation I could have to get rid of them for ever.

"You look great, Frankie," said Monty B, coming over. "But not as good as me in my tutu! And don't forget," he whispered, "if Polly gives you any more trouble – I'm your man!"

"Oh, yeah," I said, giggling. "She'll be dead scared of you wearing *that!*"

Eventually, Mandy and the stage manager of Arthur's play, whose name was Julian, came to some sort of agreement; he and his crew needed to get the stage ready for *their* play, but Julian promised Mandy that he would come in during the week and help get the hall ready for *ours*. He went off to have a chat with Ellie's dad who was busy rigging up lights, and Mandy grabbed some chairs to mark out an area on the floor to be our *makeshift* stage.

"Oh my God, yeah, did you see how Mandy was looking at that guy, Julian?" Neesha said suddenly. "You can tell she really fancies him."

"But how do you know she hasn't got a boyfriend already?" said Ellie, who was looking through her script for one final, last-minute practice.

"Because," Neesha went on, in the loudest voice, "I actually heard him ask her out for a drink, and she said yes. And anyway, yeah, it's obvious she fancies him or else why would she let *him* use the stage when it's supposed to be *our* dress rehearsal?"

"Right, you lot, we're starting," Mandy called out, putting an end to the conversation. "Now, I want everyone to sit down for a second and listen. First of all, I don't want ANY talking while we're rehearsing. I know we're not on the stage, but you've got to treat this as if it's the real thing. There's no time to muck about. This is our very last opportunity to practise before opening night, and we've got to use it properly."

It started off so well. We did the opening scene better than we'd ever done it, but in the next scene it all fell apart. First of all Ellie couldn't remember any of her lines, and then when she did remember them, she kept saying them in the wrong place. Like at one point Catharine said, "How did you sleep last night, Fizz-Wiz? Any nightmares?" And Ellie said, "Three teaspoons of honey, and a good squeeze of sunshine, Sabine, that's what the dream recipe says." And then they just stood there staring at each other, totally confused.

We sang *Scream!* but it was awful; really quiet and weedy. Mandy stopped us three times to do it again and again and then *again*, and I could see she was getting more and more hacked off by the minute. And then at one point, Monty B came in on the wrong side, and Mandy screamed, *"NO, MONTY! HOW MANY TIMES DO I HAVE TO TELL YOU? IT'S THAT SIDE!"* She sounded so cross, Monty B didn't even say anything back – which was a first. He just scuttled off and came back on the other side.

Julian and the guys setting up the stage for the play were making loads of noise so it was hard to concentrate, and by the time we'd finished Act One everyone was fed up and stressed. We had a quick break and then it was straight on to Act Two.

Act Two ran more smoothly than Act One and I could see we were going to get to the end, which meant I was going to have to sing my solo. I actually love the last scene because I get to grab Gobstopper and hand him over to the dream-police! But once he's been taken away, the Sweet-Dreamers run off the stage to celebrate, and I have to stay behind to sing my five lines about how scared I am that Sabine will forget me. That's it! Five lousy lines!

I was fine until the Sweet-Dreamers ran off but then my brain started to go all peculiar. I forced myself to walk forward, but my legs felt like jelly and as Mandy played the introduction, I knew it was going to be a disaster. I swallowed hard, cleared my throat and opened my mouth, but nothing came out. *Nothing!* I just stood there, opening and closing my mouth like some sort of moronic fish. All those times I'd sung it in my bedroom and it had sounded brilliant – all that believing in myself – and now this.

"Oh, Mandy, I think Phoebe's upset," said Catharine. She put her arm round me and walked me over to the piano.

"Thank you, Catharine. Sit down for a minute," Mandy called across to the others, and then she led me outside.

Standing in the corridor, Mandy leaned down and made me look at her.

"Hey, Phoebe, what's all this? Everyone gets stage fright sometimes – even me, believe it or not."

I started to cry, I couldn't help it. It wasn't just the song, it was Mum and Dad and Polly and everything.

"Don't you know that old saying? *Bad dress rehearsal, great opening night!* You're going to be absolutely fine."

"No, I'm not, you don't understand," I spluttered. "I really, really can't do it. I know I can sing. I sing all the time at home, but as soon as other people are watching me my voice gets stuck and I just can't get it out."

"Listen, Phoebe, you thought you couldn't get up on the stage and talk in front of the group that time, but you did. And you were sure you'd never be able to introduce us at our unexpected Christmas concert, but you were great."

I shook my head, still crying. I was crying so much I knew my make-up would be streaked right down my face and my freckles would be showing again. So much for my Great New Look!

"Remember what the very first leaflet said, Phoebe?"

I nodded. Of course I remembered. *Star Makers – is it your time to shine?*

"Well, it's your time to shine now, sweetheart. Just keep telling yourself that and you'll find your voice, I know you will." Mandy handed me a tissue and smoothed back my hair. "Come on, we're going to go back inside and work out the bows and encore. You'll enjoy that – it's the best bit." She gave me a big hug and wiped my eyes with her sleeve.

It was horrible walking back in. I was sure Polly gave me a funny look – like a cross between a smirk and a smile – and then it seemed to take forever to sort out the finale. We had to come on and bow a few at a time, but for some reason it kept going wrong. Finally, when everyone was on we made a big semicircle and sang, *Don't Let the Bed-Bugs Bite* for an encore. I stood on the edge of the semicircle, wishing I was in a different country or on another planet. I wondered if I could somehow fake a really deadly illness so that I didn't have to do the show at all, but then I thought about Sara and felt even worse than ever.

Once we'd changed out of our costumes and hung everything up we sat down for a chat.

"Not bad," Mandy started. "Not brilliant, but not bad. There are bits that are awesome, but I know the whole show could be like that if everyone just concentrates and gives it their all. And sorry if I was a bit ratty," she said, looking over at Monty B, "it's just that my stress levels were off the scale! Now, are there any questions?"

There seemed to be about a million questions, but finally Mandy said it was time to go and everyone charged out of the hall.

"What am I going to do, Ellie?" I groaned, while Mandy talked to Ellie's dad about the lights and stuff. "I'm going to ruin the whole show."

"What about me? I got all my lines wrong – every one!" She flopped down on a chair. "I mean did you hear me? It was a total joke."

"Yeah, but you sang your solo part brilliantly, and I bet you only got your lines mixed up because your dad was watching. I didn't sing at all!"

She pulled me down next to her. "You're going to be wicked, Phoebs. Everyone gets nervous before a show. I actually had this dream last night that I was in a school production; I think there were toads again – I don't know what that's about. Anyway, I was so nervous before I went on that I threw up over everyone – like projectile vomiting – I totally ruined all the toad costumes, but as soon as I got on the stage I was fine."

I started to giggle. Ellie's dreams just got weirder and weirder.

"Come over here a minute, Phoebe." Mandy was standing by the piano. "Why don't we sing through your song a couple of times before you go? I'm sure your dad won't mind waiting for a minute."

Ellie pulled on her coat and walked over to the door. "I'll tell your dad on the way out, Phoebs. Text you later this evening."

"Come on, Phoebe," said Mandy. "Let's get you sorted out."

I trailed over to the piano wondering how she was going to sort me out. A complete brain-transplant, maybe?

"Remember what you said just before, Phoebe, about how you can only sing when you're by yourself in your bedroom. Well, I don't want you to imagine you're in your bedroom – I want you to close your eyes and imagine you're in the dream factory. Try to imagine that you really are Lolly, about to lose your only true friend in the world."

I closed my eyes and concentrated as hard as I could. At first I couldn't see anything at all, but then out of the darkness a picture did start to appear. Not Lolly in the factory, or Sabine, or anything like that. It was Donny – wearing his snazzy white suit, grinning from ear to ear and giving me the biggest thumbs up ever.

He looked so real I could practically reach out and touch him, and as Mandy played the introduction, I opened my mouth and sang just like I'd sung all those times at home in my bedroom:

She'll be far from here, dreaming a
different dream
So far from here, forgetting how close
we've been.
Far from here, where are you now? I sigh.
So far from here, come back to me, I cry.
Oh, come back to me, I cry.

There was a loud burst of applause from behind the curtain and Julian popped his head through, still clapping.

"Wow, Mandy! Who on earth has got that fantastic singing voice? It was never you with the gorgeous freckles, was it?"

I'd totally forgotten that he was still on the stage. Mandy smiled up at him.

"A star in the making there, you mark my words. We'll all be queuing up to see her one day."

"Bye, Mandy," I squeaked, and ran out of the hall as fast as I could. I was more embarrassed than I'd ever been in my whole life – but not in a horrible way.

"Bye, Phoebe, see you on Monday," Mandy called after me. "And well done, sweetheart. You *are* a star!"

Sorting Things Out...

I was floating on air all week. Every time someone spoke to me I thought, *I'm a star in the making,* and floated right on past. On Wednesday, Polly Carter came up to me in the playground, but before she could say a word I smiled at her and turned away as though I was already a star and she was an adoring fan begging for my autograph. On Friday I floated out of school with Ellie and Sam, dreaming about my gorgeous freckles and the show and how well I was going to sing my solo, when Ellie grabbed my arm and pointed across the road.

"Your dad's here, Phoebs," she said. "Over there by that red car."

I took one look at Dad's face and came down to earth with a thump. I didn't really mind him coming to meet me but he looked so miserable that suddenly all I wanted to do was run away in the opposite direction.

I crossed the road and walked slowly towards the car, dragging my bag and scuffing my feet along the ground. "Hey, Phoebe," he said when I'd almost reached him. "I just wanted to catch you alone so we could have a chat about your show."

"What about it?" I said, suspiciously. "There's not a problem, is there?"

"No, of course not." He tried to smile but it was hopeless, and for a second I thought he was going to cry.

I walked on ahead so that I wouldn't have to look at him.

"Look, there's no problem, Phoebs," he called out, trying to catch up. "I just wanted to work out with you when I should come and see it – you know, so that it doesn't erm…clash with when Mum's coming to see it."

I whipped round, furious. "Why can't you have this conversation with Mum?" I snapped, trying not to cry myself. "I mean it's so ridiculous. Why can't you just pick up the phone and make the arrangements with Mum?" My tummy started to twist up. I couldn't believe things had got so bad that they couldn't bear to be in the same room as each other to watch their own daughter perform in a show.

"I don't want to talk about it," I said, walking ahead again. "I don't even want you to come if you can't come together."

We carried on back in silence. It was freezing cold and the sky was full of heavy black clouds. When we got to the house I tried one more time. "Look, why don't you come in and talk to Mum now." I thought about the other night after we made the costumes. "She really wants to talk to you, I know she does. If you come in now and have a cup of tea you might be able to work things out."

Dad shook his head and looked down. "It's not as simple as that, Phoebe," he said. "Look I'll call you tomorrow and we'll sort something out."

"Don't bother!" I snapped, and banged on the door.

"Go and say hello to your gran," said Mum as she let me in. "She's upstairs with Sara and she's looking forward to seeing you."

She went into the kitchen and started to get tea ready, crashing things about in one of her moods. "I just walked home with Dad," I said, following her in.

She carried on laying the table as if I hadn't spoken.

"Don't you want to know what we were talking about?"

"Not right now, Phoebe." She sighed. "You can see how busy I am. What you talk about with your dad is your own business."

"But I thought you said you still loved him? The other night when Mandy and the others were here, you said he was the only man you'd ever loved?" I was close to tears now. I just didn't get why they were both so unwilling to even try.

"I don't want to talk about it, Phoebe. One day, when you're older, I'll explain everything to you, but not now."

She turned away from me, just like she always does and something inside me snapped.

"BUT WHAT DO YOU MEAN WHEN I'M OLDER?" I screamed. I was so angry I didn't know what to do to make her understand. *"IT'S LIKE I'M OLD ENOUGH TO KNOW THAT YOU STILL LOVE DAD BUT YOU'RE TOO STUPID TO DO ANYTHING ABOUT IT. I'M OLD ENOUGH TO KNOW THAT THINGS HAVE GOT SO BAD YOU CAN'T EVEN HAVE A NORMAL CONVERSATION WITH EACH*

OTHER ANY MORE. I JUST WANT MY FAMILY
BACK, MUM. DON'T YOU GET IT?"

"STOP SHOUTING, PHOEBE!" Mum
slammed her hand down on the table making
me jump. Her hands were trembling and she
looked so old and worn out.

"Listen to me. Just listen, will you! Do you
think this is what I wanted? Dad living in
some grotty flat on the other side of town,
you stuck in your room barely able to look at
me, and Sara missing her dad so much she's
still talking to her teddies like she's a blessed
four-year-old."

I shook my head.

"I love your dad, Phoebs, but if he doesn't
want to sort things out that's his decision. I can't
make him get a job, can I? Marrying your dad
was the best thing I ever did, he's the sweetest,
gentlest man I've ever met, but he's got to take
some responsibility for this mess we're in – and
he doesn't want to hear that right now."

She turned away and leaned against the sink – as if she didn't have the strength to stand up without support.

"Come with me, Mum," I said, suddenly. I pulled her away from the sink. I didn't have a clue what I was going to do but I couldn't just stand there doing nothing. "Just come with me, will you." I dragged her towards the front door, my heart racing.

"Stop it, Phoebe," she snapped, pushing me away. "I'm really not in the mood for this. Let go of me."

"No, I won't let go! I don't care! If marrying Dad was the best thing you ever did then you've got to tell him. Just come with me."

"Stop it! I'm warning you! Let go of me!"

I yanked the front door open and pulled her out. It was stupid really – Dad was probably halfway up to the High Road by now – but I didn't know what else to do. In *The Dream Factory*, Lolly saves Sabine by calling the dream-police in secret – but it's not as if I could dial 999 and say, "Help! My mum and dad won't talk to each other and they don't realize how stupid they're being!"

I looked up the street expecting it to be empty – but I should've realized! Dad wasn't halfway up to the High Road at all. He was right there, stuck outside Number Four, talking to beaky-nose Burton. He had his back to us and Mrs. Burton was yakking on about something and nodding her head like one of those dogs that sits in the back of cars. I wanted to throw my arms round her and kiss her for being such a nosey-parker, head-nodding miracle worker.

"Dad!" I called out, and he jerked round. "Mum wants to talk to you."

I thought he'd make a run for it but he didn't. He just stood there with his hands shoved deep into his pockets. I pushed Mum towards him and went back inside to Gran and Sara.

247

I don't know what happened or where they went or what they talked about, but I was halfway through a long list of all the reasons why maybe it hadn't been such a great idea in the first place, when Mum came running up the stairs and straight into my room.

"Thank you, Phoebe," she said, her eyes bright with tears. And she pulled me into her arms for the biggest cuddle ever.

Show Time!

I was so nervous the next day I could barely eat a thing. I spent most of the morning watching the clock. Ellie texted me to say she'd forgotten all her lines, every single one, and Monty B texted me to say I should bring my dark glasses to the hall because he'd dyed his hair again and it had gone *very* wrong!

We arrived at the hall at five, got changed, and then ran through a couple of scenes and songs to warm up. Everyone was so excited and it was difficult to believe the day of the show had actually arrived after practising and practising for such a long time.

Julian had totally transformed the stage and it looked incredible. During the week he'd come in with a few guys from his work and painted the walls dark grey – covering the turquoise and the fish completely. On the back wall he'd painted a window frame with a silhouette of a city skyline, and to the side of that, an old-fashioned spiral fire escape and some tall, grey gates.

Somehow he'd managed to get hold of these manky old mattresses for us to sleep on and he'd built a special area for the Jelly-Skulls with loads of spiders' webs and eyeballs and things hanging from the ceiling.

For the scenes that took place in Baron-Von-Bolt's office he'd made a sort of extra layer of scenery, which according to know-it-all Sam was called a flat. The flat was painted pale blue with a huge, shimmery moon and lots of silver stars. There was a certificate hanging on the wall stating that Baron-Von-Bolt was President of the Dream Factory and a desk with a giant calculator for Adam to add up all his money.

It looked really professional, and not like a church hall at all.

I thought Mandy was going to cry when she saw it.

"Julian," she shrieked, practically flinging her arms round him. "You're a miracle worker. Thank you so, so much – I *love* it!"

I think Neesha might've been right about Mandy fancying Julian. I hope she was in a way, because he had to be better than Mandy's old boyfriend, the demon Declan.

When we'd finished warming up we went back into the changing room behind the stage to have a snack and something to drink. The audience were starting to come in and Mandy didn't want anyone to see us before the show started. I opened my bag to take out my water bottle, and stuck at the very bottom I noticed a small white envelope. It was a good luck card from Mum and Sara. It had a huge gold star on the front and loads of kisses inside. I knew it was sweet of them, but I couldn't help feeling sad that Dad's name was missing.

Suddenly Neesha flew in through the door.

"I swear the hall's like nearly full! My entire family is in the front row – I saw them on the way back from the loo! I've only been about fifty times! Has my make-up come off, Phoebe?"

I leaned up to pin back a strand of her hair that had come loose. "Your make-up's fine, Neesha, but how full is it, really? Are there any spaces left? How many chairs are there anyway?"

"Oh my God! Trillions! Mandy, how many seats are there in the hall?"

"Well, there are about eighty I think, but tomorrow we'll put out a few more because I think at least a hundred people are coming to the evening performance."

"Don't be nervous, Phoebe," said Catharine, putting her arm round me. "Just imagine that everyone in the audience is naked."

"Except for my nan!" said Monty B. His hair was so bright it was practically psychedelic. "The thought of her naked might really put you off your lines."

"Oh my God, yeah, and what about the thought of *you* naked," said Neesha, "that would be enough to put someone off their lunch never mind their lines!"

"Listen up, everyone," said Mandy, laughing. "It's almost time to go on. You all need to take a few deep breaths. If anyone makes a mistake, just carry on – chances are the audience won't notice. Now remember, I don't want to hear a sound while you're offstage in the wings because the audience will hear, and for goodness' sake, don't forget to smile!"

The door opened again and Arthur popped his head round to wish us luck.

"*Loving* the costumes," he said. "It's funny, but they look just like some Mrs. Beagle sold at the church jumble sale last month."

"Thank you, Arthur," said Mandy, steering him firmly towards the door and practically pushing him out. "Thank you so much."

We all started to giggle.

"Okay, shush, everyone, we're starting. Tara's mum is going to stand in the wings and make sure you all appear when you're supposed to. I'm going out to the piano now. As soon as I start playing, that's your cue to come on."

We stood in the wings, straining to hear the piano, but the only sound I could hear was my stomach churning over and over and I had to concentrate really hard not to run straight out to the loo. Then the lights went down – the hall was suddenly silent – and Mandy began to play.

We survived Act One without any major disasters. Catharine was amazing and we got a really big cheer at the end of *Scream!* A couple of people forgot their lines, but somehow we carried on.

In the interval I started to feel seriously ill. Everyone else was rushing around, excited now that the first scary bit was over, dying to get back onstage – but of course for me the scariest part was still to come. I sat down, but that was a mistake; my legs turned to jelly and I wasn't sure I'd be able to get up again before Act Two started.

"Wasn't that *amazing*?" Monty B plonked himself down next to me, practically knocking me off the chair.

"I so wish we were doing more than three performances," said Sam, coming over to us. "Adam, you were brilliant! I nearly wet myself in one of our scenes – you added loads of stuff that wasn't in the script."

"It's called improvising," said Monty B. "All the best actors do it!"

"Yeah, well it nearly gave me a heart attack. So warn me next time, will you?"

"Well you can't actually *warn* someone

you're going to improvise," Adam started to explain, but just then Mandy popped her head round the door. Her eyes were shining and she looked very excited.

"Well done, you lot! That was fantastic! Keep your energy levels up; I want Act Two to be even better. Let's talk it through. We're going back on in about five, so quieten down for a bit or you'll lose concentration."

The rest of the show seemed to race by and suddenly it was time for my solo. Somehow I walked to the front of the stage, every muscle in my body tensed up as if I was about to take part in a boxing match.

Mandy played the introduction and even though I'd heard it a trillion times before, for a second it got all confused in my head. I missed my first two lines, forgot the third and fourth, and just about managed to get out the last, before Sabine rushed on, gave me a cuddle, and the lights went down. *What a star!*

Backstage, it was chaos. Everyone was talking at once:

"Did you see me turn the wrong way in, *Don't Let the Bed-Bugs Bite*?"

"I nearly died when that telephone fell off the table!"

"The bows were brilliant. You got such a loud cheer, Sam!"

"Where are my jeans? I can't find them anywhere!"

I really wanted to join in with all the noise and excitement but I couldn't.

"Shame about your solo, Phoebe," Polly said suddenly. "Never mind, I'm sure no one else noticed." I looked around to see if any of her friends were listening, but she was by herself. I couldn't work out if she really meant it was a shame – or if she was being sarcastic, so I turned away and carried on getting changed.

"Hang your costumes up," Mandy shouted above the din. "Don't leave anything on the

257

floor, especially you Ellie!" She came over and put her arm round me. "You were fantastic, Phoebe! I told you you'd be fine."

But I knew she was just saying it because I wasn't fine at all – I was rubbish.

After a bit Gran came in to get me.

"Phoebe Franks! That was amazing. Did you hear me cheering at the end? You were SO good, sweetheart. Come here and give me a cuddle."

"Don't be so nice," I felt like saying as she pulled me close. I could feel tears start to prickle at the corners of my eyes, but I really didn't want to spoil the evening.

"Didn't you see, Gran? I missed out the first four lines of my solo, and I only have five!"

"Don't be daft, Phoebe, no one in the audience would notice something like that. All I know is that you sang and danced like a professional, and I could hear every word you said. Your grandpa would have been so proud.

258

Now come on, love, let's go home. You must be worn out."

I felt a bit calmer in the morning but I was still nervous about doing my solo. I kept telling myself that I was a star in the making and I'd said Donny's mantra about a million times. The trouble was, I didn't really believe in his stupid mantra any more than I believed in myself!

Dad rang to say he was coming to see the matinee with Sara and that he'd pick her up a bit later. I still really wanted Mum and Dad to watch the show together but Mum had already arranged to come to the evening performance by herself. It was stupid but I just had this weird feeling inside that if they came to see the show together I'd be able to sing my solo and everything would be okay.

In the end, even though I tried so hard, the matinee performance wasn't much better than the opening night. It would be difficult to describe how the music I'd listened to so many times before could suddenly sound so completely unfamiliar, but it did, and as I walked to the front of the stage I missed my entrance *again*. I just stood there doing my very best impersonation of a fish until finally my brain connected to my mouth, and the last couple of words came out. Thank goodness I *didn't* get the part of Sabine; it would have been the biggest joke ever!

In the break between the matinee and the evening performance, I noticed that Polly Carter's dad was there. Polly hadn't mentioned her new baby brother at drama or at school, and she seemed to be going out of her way to pretend her dad didn't exist either. I wanted to ask her about the baby, what his name was and stuff, but I was pretty sure she'd just tell me to get lost.

I almost managed to get *my* dad out of the hall without him talking to anyone about magic auras or hands-on healing, but just as we were about to escape through the door Monty B came bounding over to us.

"Hi, Mr. Franks," he said. "What did you think of the show? Wasn't it great?"

"Hey, Monty B, nice to see you. No need to call me Mr. Franks..."

I closed my eyes tight. Surely even my dad would realize that you can't just go round telling people that your name is Eagle Dust?

"...just call me...Rob."

I opened my eyes. Everything was normal. Monty B was chatting away, like he does, about turquoise walls and Christmas angels and stolen costumes, and then bang in the middle of a sentence he spotted his nan and went bounding off in the opposite direction.

"See you later, Frankie," he called over his shoulder, before crashing into a row of chairs and landing on his bum. He looked up from the floor and blew me a kiss, then hauled himself up and lurched across the hall.

"Crazy as ever," I said, giggling, and steered Dad and Sara out of the hall. We went to eat at McDonald's even though Dad said he wouldn't touch the food himself, but I was so hungry I ordered two burgers and a large fries.

I was halfway through my second burger when Polly walked in with her dad.

"Look, there's Gobstopper!" Sara shouted out, waving and pointing. "Hey! You were really, really good!"

"Oh, thanks," said Polly, blushing a bit, then she looked at me and smiled. "You were really good as well, Phoebe."

I was so surprised I nearly choked on my burger, but I recovered enough to smile back.

"Yeah, you were something else, Phoebe," Dad said, totally unaware that anything weird was going on between me and Polly. "You lit up the stage, you really did. It was so great to see you up there on the stage performing; I could hardly believe it was you."

I wanted to thank him for not telling Monty B that his new name was Eagle Dust, and for not saying anything embarrassing to any of my friends, and most of all for not mentioning how I'd ruined my solo, but I was still trying to get my head round the fact that Polly Carter had actually said something nice to me.

"Do you mean lit up like a Christmas tree, or something?" Sara twittered on, feeding her chips to Barney. "You know I can't wait to join myself; it's going to be so brilliant! I thought you were really good as well, Phoebs, apart from stuffing up all your lines at the end."

"Never mind about stuffing up my lines, I'll stuff my chips down your throat if you don't shut your mouth!"

"You know what, Phoebs?" said Dad. "I wish I could come and watch the show again tonight."

Sara snorted. "I know it was good, Dad, but it wasn't *that* good!"

Finding My Voice At Last

Back at the hall with an hour to go until the evening performance, I started to feel quite excited. I pushed the small matter of my solo to the back of my mind and went to find the others. Julian was there again helping Mandy put out the extra chairs. They were listening to really loud music and mucking about and when I walked past them, Julian winked at me and said, "Make way for the star of the show!"

Everyone was in the dressing room at the back, signing each other's programmes and sorting out their make-up with Tara's mum. Adam had put on Sam's costume for a joke and he was teetering about in her high heels and ultra-short mini-dress.

"Bend down! Bend down!" cried Monty B – and he stuffed the front of the mini-dress with a pair socks.

"Oh my God, Adam! I am so going to bribe you at school with this," shrieked Neesha, taking a load of photos of him with her phone.

"You're just jealous, Neesh," said Monty B. "Here, I've got some spare socks if you want them."

"As if," said Neesha grabbing the socks and then wrestling Monty B to the floor.

She was just in the process of stuffing the socks down his trousers when Mandy came in.

"Hey! What's going on? Actually I don't think I want to know, but be gentle with him, Neesha; I can't face sewing any more costumes! Oh, and Phoebe, your mum just popped in to buy an extra ticket. She's lucky because it was literally the last one available – it's standing room only now!"

I didn't even know Mum was bringing

someone and I wondered just for a second if it might be Dad. The thought of them watching me in the show together gave me the most amazing tingly feeling right down to my toes, even though I knew there was actually more chance of Mandy getting married to Arthur than of Mum and Dad sitting next to each other for more than five minutes without getting into a huge row.

"Take a photo for me, will you?" I asked Catharine, giving her my phone and I pulled Ellie and Sam and Tara and Neesha round me. Mum and Dad might not be able to sort themselves out – but I wasn't going to let that spoil my first ever show at Star Makers.

"Say 'Monty B'," said Catharine, and we all made stupid faces and collapsed on the floor, laughing. Then Monty B and Adam came over and actually sat on top of us and Catharine took another picture.

By seven-thirty the hall was packed. It was

so full some of the parents had to stand at the back, and the atmosphere was electric. Waiting to go on I felt like it was my birthday and Christmas all rolled into one and I knew there was nowhere else in the world that I'd rather be.

Mandy popped backstage just before we were due to start. She looked amazing. Her hair was black with bright, yellow tips, and she was wearing a silky yellow top, with tight black jeans and these outrageously high-heeled boots.

"Give it your best, guys. It's your last chance – just give it everything you've got."

A few moments later the lights went down and the show began.

It was so much better than the opening night *and* the matinee. I couldn't believe how good everyone was. Nothing went wrong and every song got a massive cheer. I tried to spot Mum in the audience but it was too packed and the lights were too bright. When Monty B came on wearing his pink tutu I thought I heard her laugh but *everyone* cracked up so I couldn't be sure. I was having so much fun I wanted it to go on for ever but the whole performance seemed to pass in seconds and suddenly it was time for my solo.

As I walked to the front of the stage something made me look out across the hall. It was just a feeling really. And there, through the dazzling lights, right at the back in the middle, I could just about make out Mum *and* Dad. They were standing next to each other, sort of together but separate, looking right at me, as if somehow *I* had the answer. And then as Mandy played the introduction to my song, Dad held out his hand to Mum – and without taking her eyes off me for even a second, Mum reached her hand out back to him.

It was as if everything else had been one long rehearsal leading up to this point. I looked across at Mandy and she gave me a huge, encouraging smile. I could hear all these voices in my head. Mum and Dad arguing, Sara announcing at breakfast that morning that my life was about to change, Polly saying sorry at the hospital. But loudest of all I could hear Mandy telling me that it was my time to shine. I took a deep breath, opened my mouth and without the tiniest quiver of hesitation, I sang my solo.

The audience leaped to their feet cheering wildly and a thousand sparkly fireworks exploded around the hall. Well, inside my head anyway! It was like magic. Coming on for the bows I glanced down at *my* feet to see if they were still touching the stage because I felt as if I was at the top of that mountain I thought I'd never be able to climb. I'd found my voice! Finally, after all this time I'd found my voice and I felt like a star. I wanted to fling my arms around everyone and tell them I loved them!

Mandy came onto the stage after we'd finished the encore and gave out presents to Ellie's dad, my mum, Monty B's nan, Tara's mum, and a few other people who had helped out with bits and pieces, and then she turned to us.

"My biggest thanks, of course, go to this awesome bunch of children who have been a total pleasure to work with from beginning to end. I told them when they first joined Star Makers that we were starting out on an adventure, and I hope so much that this weekend is just the first of many more exciting times together. They're all stars – every single one of them! Let's show them again how much we enjoyed the performance."

I could still hear the clapping and cheering as I got changed. And I could definitely hear Mum and Dad cheering louder than anyone else, just like when they came to see me in my school play all those years ago.

"Wasn't that amazing!" said Monty B coming over to give me a hug. "And your solo was even more amazing – it was awesome!"

"That's because I'm truly gifted," I said, grinning. "By the way, did you see? My mum and dad are here *together*."

"Yeah, I know, I saw when we came on at the end. What's going on?"

"I'm not sure but I'm going out to see them now. I'll talk to you later."

"If you get the chance, Frankie, ask your dad if I can still borrow his guitar."

I stopped dead by the door and turned back. "Please tell me you're joking," I said.

"Yes Phoebe Franks, I'm joking. When are you going to get my sense of humour?"

"Erm...when you start being funny!" I said, and we looked at each other and burst out laughing.

The hall was packed with parents and grandparents milling around, waiting for their children to come out of the dressing room. Ellie and Sam were standing to the side with Adam and Neesha.

Ellie pulled me over and gave me a big hug. "You were wicked, Phoebe."

"Oh my God," said Neesha. "I swear I nearly cried when you sang your solo."

"Yeah, Ellie was right," said Sam. "You have got a brilliant voice."

Adam winked at me. "But surely not as brilliant as yours, eh, Sam."

I started to blush and giggle at the same time.

"There will be no giggling in my factory," Adam called after me as I pushed my way through the crowds to the back of the hall where Mum and Dad were waiting.

"Look who's here," said Dad, as I reached them. He smiled – a proper smile that reached all the way up to his eyes. "The star of the show."

Mum threw her arms round me. "You were fantastic, Phoebe, we were so proud of you we didn't know what to do with ourselves."

I could hardly recognize Mum. She was all dressed up in some new jeans, a lacy black top, and a pair of boots I'd never seen before. And she'd had her hair done.

"You look lovely, Mum," I said, staring at her. I couldn't remember the last time she'd made such an effort.

"Yes, you look lovely, Maxine," said Dad. "Really lovely."

I was lying on my bed later on reliving every detail of the whole evening. I smiled to myself thinking about how Monty B had sent me a text saying: *What happened after the show? R u ok? Thought I might shave my head... what do u think?* And about how I'd said goodbye to Mandy and then on the spur of the moment, without really thinking, I'd given her a quick hug and whispered, "Thank you for everything, Mandy. I love you."

And most amazing of all, about how Polly Carter had come up to me just before we left and asked me to sign her programme. And then before I could lose my nerve or run away in the opposite direction I'd said, "Look, I know you said sorry that day at the hospital about hiding my script and everything, but I still don't get why you did it. Or why you did all that other stuff."

She just stood there for a second and I was sure she was going to walk off without answering, but then she looked right at me and said, "Remember the first day at Woodville, Phoebe?"

Of course I remembered. How could I forget? Mum and Dad had just split up but decided it would be *nice* if the whole family was there to wave me off on my first day and I was so nervous I was nearly sick and Sara was going on and on about how Barney's paw was hurting and he really needed me to kiss it better.

"Anyway, I saw you standing there with your mum and dad and your sister," said Polly. "And you were just like the perfect family." She blushed a bit. "Your mum and dad looked so nice and your sister was standing there holding her teddy and I was there with my dad because, you know, my mum was in too much of a state to get out of bed that morning. And I was sure everyone knew my dad had moved in with our neighbour, Diane. And at that moment I just wished so much that I was you." She looked down at the ground and scuffed her shoe. "It's stupid, I know."

I nearly burst out laughing. I couldn't believe it. Polly Carter jealous of *me*!

"It *is* stupid," I said. "*Us* the perfect family – that's the biggest joke ever. My mum and dad had just split up as well – my dad had gone totally loop-de-loop – and Sara was driving me nuts."

"I am sorry, you know," she said. "It's just that everything was such a mess and I guess I took it out on the wrong person."

And then before I could say anything else she leaned over and gave me a hug. Polly Carter gave *me* a hug. I nearly pinched myself to see if I was awake. After I'd recovered from the shock I signed her programme, *C U at the next show, love Phoebe x*. And she signed mine, *U were gr8t, love Polly xx*.

"I'm so proud of you, Phoebe," Mum said, coming in and sitting on my bed. "You were fantastic, and I don't just mean in the show."

But I knew what she meant. She was talking about the other day. I still don't know what happened exactly, when Mum and Dad went off up the road – but whatever it was it had brought my family back together, for now at least. Like I said, they don't call me Phoebe Franks Super-Sorter for nothing.

"What's the next production going to be?

Has Mandy told you yet?"

"I'm not sure, Mum. She did say something about it but I was so excited I wasn't really listening properly."

"You do want to carry on at Star Makers, don't you? It's done you the world of good. It really has."

I glanced up at my poster of Donny. I couldn't stop smiling: a great big sparkly Razzle Dazzle smile. Of course I was going to carry on. Joining Star Makers Drama Club was the best thing I'd ever done. And Mystic Sara was right after all; something did happen to me that day – and it did change my life.

For ever.

Read on for a sneak preview of the next book about the brilliant Star Makers Club, coming soon

Polly Plays her Part

Star Makers Club

"*My name is Polly and I'm here today, to say my name in a rapping way!*"

That's one of the games we play at Star Makers – the drama club I go to on Saturdays. It's called the rapping name-game and it's really cool, but if I was playing it right now I'd change the words and say:

"*My name is Polly and I'm here tonight,*

sleeping at my Dad's and ready for a fight!"

I didn't want to sleep at Dad's. But I didn't want to sleep at Mum's either. Maybe I could sleep somewhere in the middle, like at number 19. I swear no one believes me when I tell them that my mum and dad live only seven houses away from each other; Dad and Diane at number 11 and Mum at number 25. Seven houses – or fifteen giant strides – or forty-eight pigeon steps where you put one foot down exactly in front of the other; heel touching toe.

So I was sleeping round at Dad's. Or *not* sleeping as the case may be. It was impossible to get to sleep because the stupid baby was crying. Dad's *new* baby. Except he wasn't crying any more he was screaming. It was so loud Mum could probably hear him down the road at hers.

"Diane! I can't find his dummy!" Dad hissed from their bedroom. *"You know I'll never settle him without his dummy."*

I heard Diane get up and shuffle around the bed to the cot.

"Hang on a sec, Simon, I'll find it."

The screaming got louder. I could imagine the baby's face screwed up like an old tissue.

"Here it is, Jakey-boy," said Diane, in her soppy *talking to the baby* voice. And the screaming stopped.

It's like magic you know," said Dad, yawning. "It's just like waving a magic wand."

I lay in bed for a bit longer as the house grew quiet again thinking about the magic wand *I'd* like to wave – the one that would get rid of Diane and *Jakey-boy* for good. After a bit when I was sure Dad and Diane were asleep I got up and turned on my new laptop. Dad bought me the laptop when he moved in here. It was supposed to make everything okay – leaving Mum, moving in with Diane, having a new baby. Like getting a new computer could make up for all of that!

The screen glowed in the dark as I pulled on an old sweatshirt and sat down ready to tap in my secret password. There were all sorts of sites Dad had forbidden me from going on, particularly social networking sites, but I wasn't that bothered about chatting to a bunch of strangers anyway. I searched around for a bit until I found this game called **THWACKERS** where you have to eliminate the bad guys before they eliminate you. I played for ages and by the time I logged off I'd scored so high I was third on the leader board.

"**WELL DONE**," the computer flashed. "**YOU HAVE SUCCESSFULLY ELIMINATED ALL YOUR ENEMIES!**"

Diane was making pancakes when I went down in the morning. Dad had told her once that I love pancakes and ever since then she makes them whenever I stay over.

"Morning Polly," said Dad. "You look shattered. I hope Jakey didn't wake you. We couldn't find his dummy."

Jake was propped up in his high chair. As soon as he saw me he started to bang his plastic spoon on the tray and then he flung it on the floor and reached his arms out. He does that whenever anyone walks in so it's not as if he was especially happy to see *me* or anything.

"I'm going home to Mum's straight after breakfast," I said, sitting as far away from Jake and his sloppy breakfast as I could get. "She's taking me out to get new school shoes."

Dad glanced at Diane. "She didn't say anything about that," he said, frowning. "We were going to go down to the park later. Jakey's really looking forward to it, aren't you Jakey?"

He put his face right into Jake's and gave him a big slobbery kiss. Jake squealed in delight and banged his spoon even harder.

"He's only eight months old, Dad. I don't think he understands stuff like, *looking forward to things*. And anyway, I'm too old to *play* in the park."

"He looks forward to seeing *you*, Polly," said Diane, handing me a plate piled high with pancakes. "His eyes light up every time you walk in the room. You must've noticed. We *all* look forward to it," she added. "Don't we Simon?" Dad nodded but he didn't take his eyes off Jake, not for a second.

Diane's always saying nice things like that to try and get me to like her. Honestly, it's desperate. She goes on and on about my green eyes as if they're really special - and she says other stupid stuff like, "You're lucky being so slim, Polly," and, "Oh, I'd love to have black hair like yours, it's so dramatic!" She's really young, years younger than Mum, and she's got this crazy idea that we're going to end up best friends or something.

"I don't actually like pancakes any more," I said, pushing my plate away. "Can I have some cereal?"

Diane sighed and passed my pancakes

across to Dad. I knew I was being stroppy but I didn't care. I'm always stroppy round at Dad and Diane's – *looking for a fight*, Dad says – but it's not like *I* started it!

I walked back home very slowly. Pigeon steps – heel to toe, heel to toe. I passed number 13, then 15, 17, 19, 21 and 23. All the odd numbers. Maybe if we lived on the other side of the road where all the numbers were even my *life* might be a bit more even. I mean everyone knows how totally *odd* it is to fall in love with someone who lives in the same street as you.

"Have you heard about Polly Carter's dad?" all the neighbours were saying when it happened. "He's only gone and moved in with Diane at number 11!"

I hung about outside Mum's for as long as I could. We weren't really going to get new school shoes – I just couldn't face spending the day with Dad and Diane. And I'm not too old to go to the park either; I'm only in Year Seven. It's just that whenever we go anywhere together, me, Dad, Diane and the baby, I know people are staring at us and whispering behind their hands.

"Poor Polly," they're probably saying. "Pushed aside to make way for the Great Baby Jake."

Suddenly the front door flew open and Mum came charging down the path.

"Hey! Watch it!" I yelled, jumping out of the way just in time.

"Polly! What on earth are you doing here? You scared me half to death."

She was dressed-up really smart in a dark-grey suit and high heels and she'd blow-dried her hair.

"You're supposed to be over at your dad's aren't you? Oh never mind – listen, I can't stop. Make yourself something for lunch and I'll see you later."

She swept past me, her hair flying out behind her. I watched her all the way to the top of the road to see if she'd look back and wave or something but she shot round the corner and disappeared. It was totally weird to see her all glammed-up and rushing off so early in the morning. She's hardly been out since Dad left. She spends most of the time cleaning the house; scrubbing away for hours on end. And *I* spend most of the time tiptoeing around her as quietly as I can – doing my best to keep out of the way.

It was almost the end of the Easter holidays and I felt as if I'd spent the whole break going up and down the road from Mum's to Dad's and back again.

Look out for the next books about the sparkly Star Makers club, coming soon.

For more fabulous fiction, check out www.fiction.usborne.com